Liss Court

STAR-CROSSED SERIES

WRITTEN BY

BELLE RONDEAU

LIS'S COURT
STAR-CROSSED SERIES

In no way is it legal to reproduce, duplicate, or transmit any part of this document electronically or in printed format. Recording of this publication is strictly prohibited and any storage of this document is not allowed unless with written permission from the publisher. All rights reserved.

This book is a work of fiction, and all characters, places, events, and names are the product of this Author's imagination. Any resemblance to other events, locations, or persons, living or deceased is purely coincidental. The Author reserves all rights to be recognized as the owner of this work.

The information provided herein is stated to be truthful and consistent, on that any liability, in terms of inattention or otherwise, by any usage or abuse of any policies, processes, or directions contained within is the solitary and utter responsibility of the recipient reader. Under no circumstances will any legal responsibility or blame be held against the publisher for any reparation, damages, or monetary loss due to the information herein, either directly or indirectly.

Respective authors own all copyrights not held by the publisher. The information herein is offered for informational purposes solely and is universal as such.

Copyright © 2023 Isobel Rondeau

In time we grow

In time we smile

In time we love

In time we grieve

In time we heal

We never forget

Forever in our hearts

J, T, D, M

CONTENTS

PROLOGUE vii

1. Lis 1
2. Lis And The Wolf 10
3. Gavin 21
4. Apollo 25
5. Lis 31
6. Rhea 35
7. Lis 41
8. Kadz 43
9. Rhea & Apollo 45
10. Lis 48
11. Katz & Lis 51
12. Gavin 54
13. Rhea 57
14. Lis And The Pack 63
15. Gavin & Kadz 70
16. Rhea & Lis 72
17. Lis & Kadz 80
18. Lis-The Change 87
19. Kadz & Madi 97
20. Lis 99

21.	Apollo	112
22.	Rhea	116
23.	Kadz	118
24.	Lis & Madi	123
25.	Gavin & Lis	128
26.	Lis	133
27.	The Baby	145
28.	Lis's Court	157

EPILOGUE 169

PROLOGUE

The girl was the answer. She needed to be put in Gavin's path. How could we do that?

His mother and I had avoided disaster after disaster that had befallen this world. Had we made the right decision? Ian and Enid were happy and, on their way to lead the Caprica World and guard the doorways to the worlds beyond them. Tyler and his new bride, Lis, were unavailable now that the curse that followed her family was broken. Freedom was learning about his heritage and learning to rewrite his family chant book. Apollo had his hands full leading his lycanthrope pack and keeping his true self hidden from those he loved. Gavin was headstrong and willful, not unlike his mother. Would he ever be the God we knew he could be? Would love help to guide him? We wondered endlessly if our youngest child would ever grow up. He needed Lis as much as she needed him. We just needed to put them together.

Where would Lis and her mother, Rhea, fit in with this bunch of misfits? I shook my head slowly as I watched Lis and the path she had been led to. Where would she go, I wondered, and how many choices would be laid before her on her quest to find herself and claim her court of choice? Let's start there…

CHAPTER ONE

Lis

I hated being a teenager. When I grew up, I was going to have my own swimming pool. The heat today was unbearable, like living inside a dam oven turned on high heat.

Like any other day, the sun was high in the sky. Its waves of heat bounced off the black asphalt and sent little swells rippling in the air. The tall trees looked like they were moving but it was only the tiny heat waves rippling around them. The relentless sun beat the high white clouds scurrying away to try and fight another day. I watched listlessly as the red mercury rose higher and higher in the thermometer minute by endless minute. I lounged on the swinging porch chaise, the fluffy cream-colored cushions wilted under the heat and my burning body. My hair piled high on top of my head in a messy bun felt like a toque trapping the heat within the mass of red curls. Even dressed in my newest rose-colored summer sleeveless dress I was hot. Period. I could almost feel the freckles popping out on my damp warm skin.

My mind wandered back to this morning when it was a bit cooler. I watched my mom, exhausted, get home from her long night shift at the hospital. Her dark auburn hair had been plastered against her head; her eyes almost closed before reaching the bottom of the stairs. A quick hello and goodnight before she enclosed herself in the only room that had the barest chill from the little air conditioner we owned. I listened as it rumbled overhead. I hoped it would keep her cool enough that she could get a few hours of sleep before she had to leave again. I had been happy for her when she graduated from nursing, I hadn't known it would take her from me so often. I missed our chats; they had been happening fewer and farther in between the last few months. She had promised me years ago that our lives would be better if she had a better education. I dammed the man who had left us, my father, who I barely remembered except for his loud voice and the one who had dealt out the punishments. My last failure had been spilling my iced tea on the kitchen table, being ripped from my chair, and receiving a spanking like I had not ever had before, making me scream until I had been told that yelling would only make it hurt worse. I had quieted and then cleaned up the spill with the towel my mom had handed me. She had poured me a bit more juice and my father asked why she would waste it on me because I was barely able to function, stupid as I was. My mom had told him then to shut up and not speak about me that way, he raised his hand to slap her, as he had done many times before, but this time I suppose she had had enough from him. This time, she had thrown the pitcher half filled with sticky iced tea right into his face. The knife in her hand seemed to come out of nowhere. She told him to leave the house and never come back again. That man, coward that he was, left, screaming that he would pay her back for being so ungrateful. We hadn't heard a peep about him since that day. I never missed him, and hardly ever thought of him. I made up stories when asked about where he was or if he was around. Rodeo Cowboy was a good one, no one asked more questions when I said that. It was just my mom and myself and always had been for all the important dates in my life. I had no grandparents, that I knew of. The elderly neighbor said I could call her Gramma, but I liked calling her Artemis, it was her name after all.

My daydreaming came to an abrupt stop when I heard a sound at the back of the house, but I stayed put. It was just too hot to move and go check it out. The silence around me was welcomed. The hum of the air conditioner and the fridge, the grandfather clock ticked loudly inside the house. I wished we had the money to get a pool, maybe when I graduated high school, one more year left, and finished university, I would get an excellent job and look after my mother like she had for me, but I would get her a pool. Slowly I wiped my hand on the cushion, how on earth do you get sweaty palms? I heard the noise again. Oh man, I did not want to move. It was probably just the wind slapping at the old wooden screen door. Except there wasn't any wind. Just the heat. Even the flies had retreated from the heat. Probably making a fly nest under the porch where it might be a few degrees cooler. I heard the creak of the wooden steps, the second one from the bottom, it had squeaked my whole life. I tended to skip over that step just so I wouldn't make any unnecessary noise. I knew no one else but my mom and I were there, had she woken up so soon, it must have been too hot in her room.

"Mom." I called softly, "I'm on the porch, why are you up so early?" my voice sounded too loud to me even though I had barely raised my voice.

"Moooom, Helloooo" I called again a bit louder in case she hadn't heard me. But still no reply.

I supposed I should go check it out. Slowly dragging my legs over the edge, I stood up and breathed in a deep breath of stifling air. Maybe I would put my head in the freezer for a few seconds to cool it off. Yup, that sounded like a promising idea, maybe there would be some ice cubes I could suck on one to cool my insides as well. Looking forward to that I reached for the handle on the front screen door. I loved that this house was so old. My mom said I was an old soul, whatever that meant. I liked olden-day things; I liked the stories that came with old stuff. This house was over one hundred years old. Everything was wooden inside. My mom said the house would be standing long after we left this earth. I wondered if I would have kids and they would have kids and this house would one day be their home as well. In my mind, I pictured several yelling, laughing red-haired children racing about the house and yard. Chasing after a large, white, long-haired dog which drooled as he waited anxiously for the children to catch up to him before he took off racing down the black driveway, I knew he would stop just before the road. I smiled. Had I mentioned I was a dreamer? My mother was a realist, and I was a dreamer. I loved books, preferring them to the movies made now. Actors, no matter how good, would never match up to my mind's picture of the heroine or hero. I stepped further into the house; it was too quiet. I couldn't hear my mother banging around in the kitchen, she would be eagerly looking for caffeine if she had woken up.

"Hello, who's there?" I asked again, in a more forceful voice. Had some stranger thought they could just enter the house and help themselves to our food, then I quickly thought I could help them with a cold glass of water before sending them on their way again, we weren't a halfway house or anything like that. But it was hot out, and water would help anyone.

I thought I heard a soft moan, was the person in pain or were they just happily drinking all the cold iced tea? Quietly, I picked up the heavy silver candle holder from the hall table and holding it high above my head I entered the kitchen. No one was there, however, the cupboard with all the glasses was open and there was an empty glass beside the sink. So, it was an iced tea-drinking thief. Then I remembered the squeak of the second bottom stair. My mom was up there innocently sleeping away. I walked quickly to the stairs and stepped up, remembering to skip the second one. Too late I remembered that I had left my phone on the swing outside. Well, I had to go and at least try to save my mom. I heard glass clinking together, my mom's perfume bottles. What were they looking for? We had no money that I knew of, no expensive jewelry, and even the car my mom drove was ten years old and made grinding noises when she braked too hard. I smelled wet dog as I came to the top of the stairs, which was weird, we didn't have any pets. I stepped slowly to the old, white-painted door and reached out to push it open. It slid open not making any noise. My eyes adjusted to the darkness, and I saw a hulking figure standing at my mom's huge dresser. The person was looking intently at something and didn't realize I had entered the room. The silver candlestick was still gripped tightly in my hand, I must have made a little startled noise because the figure slowly turned towards me. I saw them raise a hand and cover their lips with their pointer finger. Be quiet! They wanted me to be quiet in my own house. The stranger took a quick look at my still-sleeping mom and made one step toward me. I raised my candlestick and pointed back at the person. Then gestured them to proceed me out of the room. Quietly the figure stepped out into the hallway. I glanced at my mother's still form and swallowed my fear. I turned and stepped out of the door and softly closed it behind me. The person had started down the stairs, and I figured I should follow and make sure they left the house. I also reasoned that if they had wanted to harm us, they would have done so by now.

At the bottom of the stairs, I replaced the candlestick and looked for the first time at the hulking man who had been in my mother's room, looking through her things although only after having a cold glass of iced tea and placing the glass beside the empty sink. That was kind of weird. I wondered what they had been looking for.

"Who are you? What do you want and why were you in my mother's room? How do you know where things are in my house?" the questions tumbled out of my mouth as I looked over the stranger. I noticed the low hip-hugging jeans, worn in all the right places, fit him like a glove, the tight black t-shirt that outlined the ripples of his stomach. He had no shoes on. That would have been a tough walk across the blazing hot black asphalt. His shaggy black hair curled around his shoulders. I stopped at the piercing green eyes that were hooded by his dark eyebrows, watching me as I watched him. My breath caught, had I ever seen a more gorgeous creature?

"Hello, you must be Lis. My name is Gavin. Your mom invited me to stop in today. I thought she must still be sleeping, I smelled eucalyptus and had to find where it was coming from. I wasn't sure you would be home. It's nice to finally meet you." His voice was deep and clear, friendly.

His voice rolled with quiet laughter, was he laughing at me? I bristled and stood up as tall as I could, five foot eight was not small for a teenager and yet I still felt dwarfed by his size, his shoulders almost the width of the doorway. My head barely came up to his chin. I jutted my chin out and raised my eyes to his before I answered him.

"I am Lis, how do you know about me, yet I have no idea who you are? I think it might be best if you left our house. I will let my mother know you stopped by Gavin." My voice was barely raised above a whisper in deference to my still-sleeping mother, I gestured towards the front door.

I watched as he passed by me, ya those were some nice-fitting jeans. How on earth could he be wearing jeans in this weather was beyond me. I felt like a wilted flower while he looked cool as a cucumber. At the doorway, just as he placed his hand on the scarred wooden door, he looked over his shoulder at me and looked from my wilted hot hair right down to my pink-painted toenails. Slowly. Then he raised his beautiful eyes back up to meet mine. A slow smile graced his red lips like he was happy with what he saw, and he gave me a small nod before he pushed the door open. I had barely seen him take the step outside and it was like he vanished.

I raced to the door to look where he had disappeared. My head swiveled left and right. Nothing. Where did he go? People didn't just disappear. I heard a loud howl. Wolves in the daytime, well that was weird. I knew Gavin was a human, after all a ghost wouldn't have drunk the iced tea. A vampire wouldn't be out in this heat, and it was daytime. Maybe a sorcerer…that was a thought. I hadn't read much on witchcraft. I would look it up as soon as I got my phone. Strolling over to the swinging chair…wait, no wind, why was the chair swinging? Was he an invisible person? Watching me race around while he swung innocently in my chair.

"Hey Gavin, are you an invisible person?" I questioned the empty chair quietly.

No response, just the quiet, the leaves crinkling on the trees from lack of water in this heat. I momentarily wished for a cooling rain, to feed the animals, to feed the browning grass, the wilted flowers, and every garden on earth. Well, I guess Gavin wasn't an invisible person, I sank into the plush cushions and looked at my phone. Dead battery, well that figures. As soon as I had something to look up it decided to die.

Getting up once more I went inside to get my charger from the kitchen. I might as well get a drink and go pee before I went back outside to let the house be quiet for my still-sleeping mom. The charger was always where it was left, beside the fridge on the little shelf that had no function that my mom and I could think of except to hold our cell phones while they charged. I poured a glass of iced tea and made a new pitcher since it would be gone by dinner, I was so thirsty today.

Putting my glass down I went to the little broom closet-sized bathroom off the back porch. We needed central air conditioning. I loved the old house, but some new appliances wouldn't be a bad idea. Of course, as quickly as I thought it, I dismissed the idea. No money, well not enough for splurging anyway. My mother had been saving for my University since the day she started her first job. I knew every dollar was thought about and where it should be spent. I was being petty, we had everything we needed to live. We didn't need extras. I quickly finished in the bathroom and washed with cool water, splashing some on my arms and face to cool me a bit before I went outside. The old rusty pipes groaned with use, and I quickly turned the taps off. I barely glanced in the mirror, but I stopped and cringed when I did get a look. My face was red, my hair a wild mess of curls with limp tendrils falling out in little groups and sticking to my neck. I looked down at the new dress and groaned, no bra (too hot) no socks (too hot) the fabric clung to my legs like they were static and outlined my breast…was that my nipple? Oh no, how terrifying I must have looked to the large imposter who had looked me up and down. I groaned aloud and hoped I never had to see that gorgeous guy again. I could have pranced around naked for all my dress was covering up. What was my mother thinking to invite him here? I wondered how she knew him, while he was older than me, he was definitely too young to be dating my mom. Maybe the wolf I heard earlier had grabbed him and taken him to its den to eat. No, that was gross, and I shouldn't think about real people like that. Sorry Universe, I silently sent out the apology.

I grabbed my iced tea and headed back to the front porch swing, now sitting there idly, with no movement of any kind. I looked once again around the vast expanse of farmland around our old farmhouse. I did love this place, it was where I had been brought up, as far as I knew this had been my home since I had left the small community hospital where I had been born seventeen years ago, almost eighteen, I corrected myself. Although it would just be another day for me and my mom, we had decided to stop celebrating our birthdays a few years ago when one birthday not one person had attended my party. I had been eight and had cried for days, asking all the friends I had invited why they hadn't shown up. I got the same response from all of them, they had been busy that weekend with their family obligations. What eight-year-old says obligations without help from an adult? My mother always made sure we had a full supper, whatever I wanted, for the one day of the year but we never called it a birthday celebration again. No presents, no balloons, no friends gathered round a birthday cake singing a useless song. Ahhh, it was too hot to think of non-birthday celebrations. I would rather think about the gorgeous stranger who entered my house and those green eyes. I closed my eyes and daydreamed a little before falling into a heat-induced sleep where those green hooded eyes followed me about. Who was he and where did he disappear to?

CHAPTER TWO
Lis And The Wolf

Hours later, I opened my eyes to the late noonday sun. How had it gotten hotter than this morning? I felt more tired than I had earlier, but I knew my mom would be getting up soon and she would need coffee no matter how hot it was outside. I had tried to get her to try iced coffee, but she poured it down the drain, coffee was meant to be hot she had said. Groaning a little at having to move in the heat I picked up my empty glass and headed inside.

The coffee was soon silently filling the glass carafe the smell wafting out and filling the kitchen with its rich pungent odor. I loved the smell of coffee. I didn't drink the stuff, but I loved how it smelled, it was how my mom smelled to me. Eucalyptus and coffee, it was the best combination in the world. I listened with a coffee cup in my hand, my mom would smell the coffee and like a zombie make her way down the stairs with her eyes closed finding me by smell. I wondered if she would ever fall but she never has. The coffee would be finished within a minute and sure enough, I heard her bedroom door open and her light steps overhead. I pictured her graceful hand gripping the old wooden banister as she made her way down. I smiled as she appeared in the kitchen doorway, a smile on her lips. My day has started.

"You are my precious doll; do you know that Lis?" she floated toward me on the most petite feet I had ever seen. Her eyes still closed she reached toward the strong smell of coffee. I poured the coffee into the mug I had been holding and handed it to her with a laugh.

"Good Morning Mother, you are my little doll too," I answered as I watched her glow with the first taste of black coffee.

"Mmmmm, so good, thank you, Lis." Little by little I watched as a transformation came over her. The stretch of her long neck, the hunch of her shoulders as she shivered with coffee love, the little shake she did right before she stood up on her toes to stretch and raised her head to look for the sunshine that filtered through the curtains above the kitchen sink window. In awe I wished for the day I would ever be as beautiful as her, even after just waking up she was magazine model perfect. Her hair was mussed perfectly from sleep. Her lashes fluttered as she got ready to open them for the first time since waking up. I smiled at her so she would see me smiling as the first thing she saw in her day. I waited for a breath more before she opened her large coffee-colored eyes and smiled at me. Her pink lips turned up in the most beautiful smile I had ever seen. Her bright white teeth filled her smile perfectly.

"I have the perfect daughter," she grinned as she took another sip, not blowing on her coffee to cool it before it filled her mouth. Just heat, I got sweaty just watching her drink the hot liquid.

"What have you been up to today?" she questioned me.

I remembered the guy; I had dreamed of. The tilt of his lips as he smirked at me and of his laughing green eyes.

"Gavin stopped by today, who is he?" I watched as her hand shook a little as she heard his name. She kind of growled and her eyes squinted as she muttered his name, her breath hitched seconds before she covered her reaction.

"Oh, I didn't realize he would stop by today, I should have been awake to introduce you both. What did he say he wanted?" she stumbled out.

"He didn't really say anything, but he helped himself to some iced tea and went to your bedroom. He said he smelled eucalyptus and wanted to see where it came from. I sent him away as soon as I could. Who was he mom and why was he in your bedroom? He seemed awfully comfortable in these surroundings. Are you dating him? He seems a bit young for you." I needed to hear her answers.

"He is just a friend from work Lis, don't worry about it. We aren't dating. I need to go shower and get ready for work. Would you please fry up the chicken in the fridge and make some rice? I will take the leftovers for lunch tonight. Thank you for the coffee, it's the best part of my day, knowing you love me enough to have it ready every morning, well afternoon I suppose." She finished the sentence over her shoulder as she walked quickly out of the kitchen.

Well, that didn't answer much, except they weren't dating, and he worked at the hospital. I would ask more pointed questions at the dinner table. Walking over to the fridge I opened the door and rooted around for the chicken. My mind thinking outlandish thoughts about the green-eyed god. I had forgotten I was going to look up wizards maybe I should widen the search and look up gods as well. Hmmm.

A few minutes later, the chicken sizzled in the frying pan with chopped-up onion and zucchini, the water bubbling in the pot waiting for the rice to be added. I chopped a bit of lettuce and cucumber and one overly ripe tomato and made a quick salad. My mom loved a salad with every meal. I hoped she would hurry; the salad would wilt in this heat in a few minutes. As if on cue, I heard her steps on the stairs once again.

"It smells delicious Lis; you are my saving angel. I would starve without you. Do you need any help?" she questioned as she danced over to the stove to smell the chicken.

"You could make the rice." I directed her as I grabbed a couple of bowls from the cupboard.

"Choose a dressing from the fridge as well. I will use whatever you do." I spoke as I filled our bowls with the crisp salad.

We danced in unspoken symmetry around the kitchen, grabbing clean plates and cutlery. The napkins and salt and pepper found their way to the scarred wooden table. Clean glasses filled with ice cubes and the pitcher of iced tea in the center. In a matter of minutes, we were both seated and enjoying our first bites of salad. We ate in silence. My mom cleared that up when we were done, placing the dirty dishes in the sink while I finished with the chicken and filled our dinner plates. Once we were seated again, I started with the questions.

"So, mom, the guy. Who was he? Why did he come here so early in the day if you work with him? He should have known you would be sleeping, that's kind of rude on his part, wouldn't you say?" Not one to beat around the bush, I knew I had to question my mom directly or she would find a way to change the subject.

"Oh Lis, he is just an intern, learning to be a doctor. I am not sure why he was here so early or what he wanted. I did invite him to visit but I didn't know he would be coming today. Just forget about him. I am going to tell him not to visit again unless I am up." Her eyes looked into mine for a minuscule second before she looked back to the chicken on her plate.

"Should I be scared that he knew your eucalyptus scent and the way to your bedroom? He knew where the glasses were and that we liked the dirty dishes on the right side of the sink. When he left, it was like he disappeared. I didn't see any footprints; I didn't hear a vehicle when he came or when he left. Why would he have just come into the house uninvited through the back door? Is there more to the story here Mom?" I questioned her again.

"Look Lis, I have some things to work out, adult things. You do not need to worry about that kind of stuff. Let me be the adult, at least for one more year. It would be best if you were concentrating on your last year of high school. Dances and boys. The Prom. The Valedictorian speech."

Her voice rose on the last comment as if she wanted to ask the question outright. Her hope that I would be Valedictorian and earn a scholarship to university was high on her list of hopes for me. I suppose I should be concentrating on that as well. A good education was costly, and every dollar awarded would be a bonus for her, and me as well.

"Okay, mother. I get the point, you adult, me lowly teenager." I grumbled.

"It's not like that Lis; you know I adore you more than anything. And I appreciate how brilliant you are. There are some things I need to take care of so we can be set for the rest of our lives. We will grow old here in our old house, together like two peas in a pod. You are my absolute best friend and I love you but today; for this conversation just let me be the adult, okay?"

She had placed her fork on her plate and held my hand as she spoke; I heard her words loud and clear.

"Okay, but I just wanted to let you know I thought Gavin was the most gorgeous person I have ever laid eyes on. I wished I had known someone might be visiting, I would have at least put a bra on." I groaned as I told her the story of our meeting and the look he had given before he left.

"Well, no need to worry, he probably won't be visiting anytime soon honey." She replied as she finished her dinner and began to clear the table.

I got up to help while she filled her lunch containers with the leftovers. I filled the sink with hot soapy water and let the dishes soak while I wiped the table down. Pouring us each a last glass of iced tea, I placed the empty pitcher by the sink.

She followed me to the front porch and sat on her favorite chair while I headed to mine. We talked about trivial things then, just a conversation about the patients she had the night before, the doctors and nurses who cared for them. I told her about a new book

I had started. It was extra reading for the IP English class I would be starting. She was a great listener. I suppose that is why she was a great nurse. Ever practical while I submerged myself in books, my fantasy worlds.

She commented that a new surgical doctor had just come on to the hospital staff. That caught my attention. I thought it was a little bit weird, why did our little general hospital need a new surgeon? Usually, the patients were sent out to the big city for major surgery. I asked her a bit about him.

"Well, he is so smart. Obviously, he is a surgeon. He seems in exceptionally good health. Youngish for a surgeon." She started.

"Hold on Mother" I interrupted, "I mean is he good-looking, is he old, does he have a family, is he bald? I do not need to know if he is in good health" I laughed at her and I did not miss the pink tinge in her cheeks as I teased. Sometimes I wished my mom would date and pretty soon I would leave for school, I worried about her being all alone. Especially on movie nights. She loved old movies.

"He is about fortyish, dark curly hair. He is single, and there isn't anyone he calls regularly. He has been at the hospital for about a month now. We had a coffee break together last night. He is very proper and extremely polite. He has the oddest eyes. They change color with his mood. Not that he's moody but it is probably stressful being a new doc in an old hospital. He is quite tall, taller than me, he must be well over six feet. He does not wear glasses, he doesn't smoke, he keeps his face free of hair. You would like him, Lis. Maybe I will invite him for a BBQ soon. Would you be ok with that?" she finally questioned me on her last breath of air.

I looked at her quietly for a moment, digesting all the information she had just dumped on me. She liked this new surgeon. However, she hadn't mentioned his name yet. I wonder if she just called him doctor. I laughed internally.

"Yes Mother, I think I would like to meet the new surgeon," I answered her with a smile. "So did he tell you, his name?" I questioned.

"Yes, it's Apollo, if you can imagine that. He looks like a Greek god and his name fits the bill. Apollo was the son of Zeus and was the god of music, the sun, poetry, and medicine. He was also a twin, I am not sure Doctor Apollo has a twin, he does have brothers though. One is named Tyler, and another is Ian. They live in Europe, I think. I don't know everything about him and that is why I wanted to invite him for dinner one night. To learn a bit more about him. He seems genuinely nice he is so polite to all the staff. He seems a bit overqualified for our little hospital, but I won't argue that we needed him." She abruptly stopped talking.

"Mom? You, okay?" I asked her.

"Oh ya, I'm okay. Just a little over tired. I should get off to work. I really hate leaving you, you know that right? But soon I will be on the day shift, and we will have proper dinner together every night for a week. I will let you know if Apollo accepts my dinner invitation. Keep your phone handy and charged. Lock the doors and windows too, okay? I'm sorry Gavin barged in here today. I will take care of it tonight when I see him." She gracefully got out of the chair and took her empty cup inside with her.

I had just about forgotten about that beautiful green-eyed guy. So glad my mom had to remind me of him again. I closed my eyes and daydreamed about him. Where had he come from, our town is quite small so almost everybody knew each other and if someone new came along the town knew about it before the person could stop at the little bakery for a coffee. Tomorrow while my mom slept, I would head into town for some groceries and a little investigation. I could learn everything I needed to know by asking Bessie at the store. She had eyes like a hawk, and everyone talked to her. She would know if anyone new was in town. I also wondered why we had a new surgeon and when did our hospital start taking on interns. I heard my mom gathering her stuff, I heard her plastic identity badge slide across the Formica countertop and land with a soft plop into her backpack. Which probably held her lunch kit, a hair tie, her water bottle, and her wallet. Everything she needed for a night at work.

Within a couple of minutes, she was exiting the house, her hands full she kissed my cheek and said goodbye, reminding me that she would call to say good night in a couple of hours. She never missed that call. I reminded her I would be fine; I had stayed home many times before. I was just going to read a book and maybe watch a movie later on. I would make some popcorn and just hang out.

I watched from my seat on the porch as our little car trudged out the gravel driveway. Little dust motes billowing behind her. The heat from the asphalt road made the car quiver as it drove further away. Once more I was alone.

It was almost seven o'clock. The heat would start to recede soon. As soon as the sun went down the temperature should be more reasonable, and I would be able to sleep. I would go have a tepid shower and put on clean pyjamas then find a movie.

A couple of hours later I fell asleep on the couch watching a movie I had memorized the lines to. An empty popcorn bowl sat neglected on the wooden coffee table, melted butter gelling on the bottom of it.

As I slept, I dreamed of brilliant green eyes that watched me as I watched Gavin the god, turn into a large midnight black wolf. His shaggy hair billowed around him as his sharp green eyes gazed across the vast mountains. It took my mind a minute to catch up as I looked around and realized, he wasn't alone. Just steps under him on the rocky ledges were other wolves, unusual colors ranging from white to brown, black, and grey. They looked so majestic, looking out across their territory. I watched as a large black wolf sniffed the air and turned his black eyes towards me. I heard a loud deep growl come from the wolf Gavin was. The black wolf nodded his head and turned away from me. Wait this felt very real, too real. I heard a quick bark of a laugh and looked at Gavin in his wolf form. He winked at me and gave a low woof; it sounded like a caress as his eyes roamed my pajama-clad body. What was this?

Abruptly I awoke to the cool night air, I could smell the distinct clean cool mountain air as I gulped in a quick breath. That was the most intense, most real dream I had ever had. I could almost feel the black wolf's hair through my fingers as I reached out to touch Gavin. He had bumped his head into my hand, and I had jumped back a little. He growled as the other wolves had pressed closer to get a scent of me. I had the feeling they listened when he growled… wait a minute. It was just a dream, there was no such thing as humans turning into wolves. I needed to get a handle on my dreams. Some things just couldn't be true. I must have been reading too much sci-fi lately.

I took all my dirty dishes into the kitchen, checked to make sure all the doors and windows were closed, and turned off the television. I would sleep in my mom's room; her mattress was more comfortable than mine. I went to the bathroom and then washed my hands. Startled when I saw that they were dirty. Where had that come from? It had just been a dream, hadn't it?

I lay in bed looking up at the ceiling for a long time before sleep claimed me in the wee morning hours. Visions of a hunky green-eyed, black-haired wolf followed me into my dreams.

CHAPTER THREE
Gavin

The little tart. Showing her body like that in front of me. How ridiculous to think she could get any emotion from me. He was like an emotional watering can. Nothing stayed inside, it was how he liked it. He thought for a minute about her wide innocent eyes, they had darkened when he looked at her. She physically wanted him; did she even realize it?

She was a baby. The female child of the Luna werewolf, Rhea. She would be off limits, to anyone else but him. We had been waiting for her to grow up and see what she would choose. Human or Werewolf, those were her choices, he didn't even know why she had been given a choice. She should have just been born to be with him and lead a wolf pack. That was what he wanted. All he needed was a Luna wolf of his own. Lis would fit that bill if she chose werewolf.

Gavin was the younger brother to Tyler, who was the High Warlock. The younger brother to Dr. Apollo, the Alpha of his pack, and the younger brother to Ian the Gatekeeper. As the youngest brother, Gavin always got away with his infractions.

He smiled as he again thought of the little tart. She didn't even know what she was yet. Rhea had warned him to stay away from her. Apollo as Alpha had been angry and didn't take Rhea's side in this matter. So, Gavin had visited their home earlier. He had known Lis was home alone while Rhea slumbered in her bed upstairs. Lis had surprised him with her anger and fierce protection of her mom. Maybe she was just wild, unhinged even. Why would she think she could be of any security to her mom? Rhea was the fiercest she-wolf he had ever encountered, and she fit well with Apollo, the know-it-all. Rhea was actually very kind-hearted and loved helping everyone, even the humans. Although she probably overdid it a bit by being a human nurse. Weird.

Their farmhouse was really old and looked ready to fall apart if a strong wind gusted across the mountains. It had been around for a long time. It should be dismantled, and another built in its place. He hadn't seen any pictures except those of Lis. He looked at them all as he climbed the wooden stairs there were twelve school pictures with the grade captured beneath every single one of them. Rhea's daughter was a beauty. He wondered what she would look like in wolf form. She would be changing soon it was inevitable. Her mom was the second in command along with him. He briefly wondered when he would be free to start his pack, he needed it. He had been tagging along behind Apollo for years. Training to be a doctor when all he wanted was to run free across the plains into the wilderness of the mountains and lead his pack.

He preferred his Lycanthrope persona when in wolf form, he felt free, uninhibited, stronger, smarter, faster than any human. He was brother to many gods and goddesses, but he was the youngest, and they mostly treated him like an afterthought. He had no clear domain like his siblings did. Apollo was the god of animals including the mythical creatures found in many worlds. Tyler was the god of magical beings and magic. Ian was a gatekeeper to all the worlds. Ophelia was the goddess of water and caregiver to the people and lastly, there was Athena the goddess of warfare and wisdom. He had no specialty no specific title no realm he looked after, he was just the youngest. He needed more; he needed a job a real job not this doctor-to-humans stuff. He was a god he just wasn't a god of any one thing.

Sighing he scuffed his worn boot into the brown dusty road. He walked over to the fence line and thought about taking off, just running away. Then he thought of his father. He couldn't disappoint him. So, he leaned on the wire fence and watched as the animals mooed and wandered around the enclosure. It was too hot for them to be anywhere but at the watering hole.

He remembered the dream he had had the evening before. When Lis had dreamed of him and ran her hands through his scruffy hair. Did she know she was there, on the cliff with the pack? Her dreams were going to become reality and he needed to be there for it. Kadzait, or Kadz had tried to sniff her. He was looking for his mate and he was intent on sniffing around every available female. Gavin growled just remembering it. Lis was off limits. She was to be his, Apollo had agreed to this. If only Rhea would listen and let her join. Why was she trying to let her daughter be human? She wasn't. She was born to be a part of this family like he had been. Her eighteenth birthday was not far off, and he meant for her to be a part of the pack before then. If she didn't join, she would either stay human and miss out on her true family or she could change without any knowledge and that would only make her resentful towards her mother and maybe all of them also. Rhea had to know that time was running out for her to let Lis know her true heritage. Rhea was so stubborn. Apollo should just make her do what he wanted. He was the Alpha and a god; he could make her and anyone else do whatever he wanted them to do. The brothers always spoke of free will for the humans of this world but to him, it made no sense. Make them do what needs to be done. They were just humans after all.

CHAPTER FOUR
Apollo

Why are you bothering me, Tyler? Can't you fix the problems on your mountain by yourself? I thought to my brother across the telepathic connection we shared. We have our problems in each of our realms and his would not be any more important than mine.

I need you all, it's important or I wouldn't have asked brother. Came Tyler's reply.

I will let you know if we can leave. Rhea can take over if needed but it is a crucial time for us here as well. I broke the connection before he could continue to ask more of me.

Paging Dr. Apollo came a tinny voice from the ceiling speakers.

I loved the surgical aspect of the hospital. Fixing the humans who were so fragile. It made me appreciate the complexity of the universe which we oversaw. How every fiber belonged in each place. When we wove this world together so intricately how did we not realize how independent the humans of this world would be? How they would grow and accept the limited choices they had. They chose who would be the leaders of their world. They chose if they worked or not. The humans who thought they ran the world were so sure of themselves, that it was humorous and dangerous of me to think like that.

If Gavin heard those thoughts, he would decide that humans were not worthy of life. He had so much to learn, from all of us. I was his last stop before we let him go and try to make his world. He seemed to have not learned anything in the time we had spent together. I know he wanted a pack of his own, he wasn't ready to lead. He needed to understand that this world we had created needed to live. It was the best one, we had all agreed, that we had designed.

Silently I looked into the waiting room of the patient I was to operate on soon. The parents hovered around the boy; frail was the best description of him. The young man had only a slim chance of surviving and his parents were having trouble believing the nurses who had spoken to them. They demanded to speak to the surgeon, me.

They both looked up as I approached, I suppose they would have heard my leather shoes on the tiles. If I had been in my wolf form, they wouldn't have even known I was in the same room as them.

"Hello, Mr. and Mrs. Herrin. My name is Dr. Apollo, and I will be performing the surgery on your son. Please follow me into my office," I gestured for them to follow. My office is the best in the old hospital. The door proudly sported the nameplate at eye level. I walked around the brown desk covered in files and gestured for the family to sit in the three chairs provided by the office intern. We sat down and I steepled my fingers. Quietly I informed the family again what would be done to their son for him to survive and hopefully live a long life. It was going to be an exceedingly difficult and lengthy procedure. Tim would be in a long recovery if he did survive the surgery. The odds were not in his favor, but we would try all that we could.

The family sat silently and asked questions when needed. Tim sat with his head down and listened to every word and when we were done, I asked if he had any questions.

"If I don't wake up from the surgery what happens to me then?" the boy asked me directly.

His mom gasped and told him not to ask such questions that he should be positive and trust the doctors to take care of him.

"Tim," I looked at him, "If you don't wake up it means I haven't done my job as well as I should. I can't promise that you will wake up, but it would help if you thought you might wake up too. If you do wake up, I promise once you are well that you will enjoy your life much more. You won't wake up in pain from your trauma anymore. You will be able to live a good life if you choose to." I watched as he digested what I said. I needed him to believe in me, it helped.

"Okay, I'll try to wake up but if I don't, do you know where I will end up? I mean my spirit. Do you know where it goes when we die?"

It was a question I dodged from most of my patients, usually, they didn't ask me out loud though. Should I lie? I could tell him, but would he believe me, would his parents?

I couldn't tell them, instead, I replied, "I believe your spirit goes where you believe it goes. Heaven? I'm not sure where that is but if you believe in that then maybe that is your spirit's final resting spot. However, Tim, if you believe you can survive and wake up, I think that is what would be best for your spirit. Can you believe in that for the next few days?"

"I can try." He replied slowly.

"Thank you for talking with us, Dr. Apollo. We will be here next week, ready to go. Tim will also be ready to go, right kiddo?" Mr. Herrin looked at Tim as he stood and held out his hand to shake his. The family stood and turned to the door.

"See you next week," I said as they filed out the door and down the fluorescent-lit hallway of the sterile hospital.

I hoped Tim would live through the surgery, but it was his choice, he would have to choose to live or die. If he chose to live, I would bring him back and he would live happily healed with his family. If he chose to quit, to die, he would be sent to another world with his memories wiped clean and he would begin again. The humans were quite shocked when they were given this choice, however, most chose to move on. Their mortal bodies having lived a life here they were ready to move on to another life. It was strange to have this conversation with the people in limbo. I wondered what the boy would choose.

Brother? Are you busy? I heard Gavin call.

Can't you just pick up the phone to call me Gavin? I replied in exasperation.

Kadz is sniffing around Lis, you need to deal with this. Rhea needs to tell her. Lis dreamed of us yesterday. Gavin continued his inner dialogue.

I'll deal with it. I growled as I snapped the conversation off.

Why would Lis be dreaming of the pack, it wasn't her time yet. She hadn't even met any of the pack. I needed to find Rhea had she finally told her the truth. I needed to spend a bit more time with the pack if these things were going on without my knowledge.

Brother, I need you now. I heard the cry from Tyler as I stood up. I felt his fear. My stomach clenched with dread, I needed to go. Now.

Gavin, get ready to go, Tyler needs us on the mountain. I commanded.

Ready to go. I will be at the hospital in three minutes. Came Gavin's quick reply.

I lifted the phone in my office and called Rhea. She was at my door in seconds. I looked at her and noticed the frown lines and the dark circles around her eyes. She was tired, she needed a break, and I would give her one as soon as we got back.

"Take care of the pack, and my office. Gavin and I will be back as soon as we can." I instructed.

"Is there anything I can do Apollo?" she asked.

"Just look after the pack and keep Lis away from Kadz or rather keep him away from her." I watched as her eyes widened and then she frowned at me.

"What have you said to her Apollo? I told you I would tell her in my own time, She is still my daughter. You have no right..."

"Rhea, stop right there. I have every right. It's my pack. I told you I would give you time, I won't much longer. You need to tell her. I won't talk about this again, do it before Gavin and I return." I interrupted her as I stood in front of her. I hated to be this alpha, but she continued to push my limits.

"Lis asked to meet you, I told her I would ask you to dinner, a BBQ next week?" Rhea questioned.

"If we are back, we can do that. It's about time I meet our future leader." I brushed a soft kiss on her head as I walked out the door. Gavin had arrived and we needed to leave quickly Tyler was in trouble and he needed us.

CHAPTER FIVE

Lis

Another day dawned; it would be another scorcher the meteorologist said on the early morning news. My mom would be home soon. I headed into the kitchen to fry up some eggs in case she wanted to eat before she headed to bed for the day, and I left for school.

I hadn't slept very soundly the dream of those green eyes had kept me awake longer than I wanted. I shouldn't have had that little nap earlier in the day.

I heard our old car rumble up the drive, so I poured a coffee for my mom and set the table.

"Good morning honey," my mom said as she opened the door.

"Good morning, Mom. How was your shift?" I replied to her as she placed her purse and lunch kit on the counter plugged her phone into the charger by the fridge and sat it on the little shelf.

"It was good, not too busy. Oh eggs, thanks I should eat before I sleep." She placed some eggs and sliced a tomato onto her plate. Sighing loudly as she took a sip of the hot coffee. "I'm not sure how I manage to fall asleep with all the caffeine I drink."

"Mom." I rolled my eyes at her as I pointed to the can of caffeine-free coffee on the counter.

"Oh, well thanks for that." She smiled around a mouth full of eggs. "School today?" she questioned.

"Yup, and I'm going to Madi's after school and for supper. We have a project to finish up. I will be home before you leave for work tonight though."

Madi was my best friend. I didn't make friends easily, but she was just the opposite of me, she was bouncy and was friends with everyone. She knew all the kids at school right down to the preschoolers, their parents, and their grandparents. She had lived here her whole life, and she loved it.

"Okay, I will just make a sandwich or something for dinner. Thank you for breakfast. Be good. See you later bug." She gathered up her plate and coffee cup and placed them in the sink. "Goodnight." She whispered tiredly as she kissed the top of my head on her way upstairs.

"Goodnight Mom. Love you." I whispered back.

I cleaned up quickly and grabbed my school bag before heading out the door. The bus would be here in a few minutes, and our drive was long.

On the ride to school, I thought about my valedictorian speech. I should start it. It wasn't long before we graduated, and I could finally leave here and get to the big university. So many different people, people who didn't know my history or my mom's past.

I daydreamed about our lives until I heard the squeal of the tires stopping at the old high school. One more year and I was out of here. The only people I would miss were my two best friends. Madi and Gabe had known each other since birth apparently. Madi was a cheerleader, prom queen, and star soccer player. She was the first person I met here. It was an instant friendship. We both reached for the last ice cream sandwich in the school cafeteria. She let me have it. Then we sat together and have every day since. Gabe was the brain. He was also a tutor and Madi needed just a little help with science. He was also a football star. Madi asked me to meet in the tutor room one day and she was with Gabe, which was all it took to be his friend. He was kind. He was also on the Dean's list with me but only just behind. I would beat him out for valedictorian but even if I didn't it would be okay if I lost to him. He also needed the scholarship opportunity.

They were both waiting for me as the bus emptied. I had to tell them about the Gavin god I had met over the weekend. Their smiles when I reached them were infectious. They babbled on about the games they played on the weekend, his football and her soccer. The entire day people stopped us to talk with them about their games and what was next. Even Mrs. Pratt, the English teacher, asked about the football game. Lunchtime was basically a party in the cafeteria with all the students singing the school song and stopping to chat with Madi and Gabe. Most everyone took photos with them, slapped them on the shoulders, and wished them good luck for next weekend's game. Madi said she was too busy to finish our project, but we would get to it soon. Before I knew it, I was back on the yellow school bus headed home. I never had the chance to tell either of them about the stranger whom I had met.

CHAPTER SIX
Rhea

I hated the night shift. I had enough seniority at the hospital to quit doing them, but we were a team and I needed to take the shifts. We needed the money or Lis wouldn't get to go to University if she chose university.

I groaned a little as I lay in bed. I could tell Lis had been sleeping in it while I was at work. I could smell her shampoo, her perfume. It was her natural scent, and I could always smell it. Even when she was a baby, I knew she was different, but I couldn't bring myself to admit it. She was my only child, her and I against the world. Until I met Apollo, I was his second, after Gavin. He told me that Lis was the reason he had come to our town, my hospital. I had kept him away from her for so long, he had let me. He watched as she grew, sent gifts for her birthday and Christmas, and gifted her first two-wheeled bike. She didn't know. I had kept that part of me away from her so she could have a chance at being human, and no responsibilities other than her schooling. She was so smart and kind. She wasn't the leader he thought she was, she needed me, I wouldn't let her go. She was my child first, never a werewolf, she didn't even believe in those things. I hoped not anyways.

Briefly, I thought back to the day I had been scratched by Beauwolf. I thought he liked me, and we had dated but all he wanted was a partner, someone to back him up when he murdered helpless victims. He thought he could control me because he had made me. He didn't know I had some inner strength which came roaring out when I became a werewolf. It hadn't taken me long to realize what he was after. One night we were running in the mountains scaring the campers and wildlife. We came upon a cliff, and I stopped just in time, he didn't. Once I had been cleared of any wrongdoing, I hightailed it out of there and finished my schooling. An Alpha, Warwick, had been my first boyfriend at school, and he was Lis's father. She would never know that or him. He told me we mated for life once we were matched but he never took that seriously. He mated with every female he could. I am sure Lis has a few siblings in the world, but I would keep her away from all of them. She was my daughter. Better to let her think her father was a useless wanderer. Warwick didn't know about her, I left before he would know. I left with nothing; he would have smelled her inside of me if I had stayed one minute longer. He seemed to know everything I was thinking. It was eerie to have someone know everything about you. Your scent, your habits, your fears. I had been a city girl so I left for the country, a place he wouldn't think to look for me. It had been life-changing just like raising a young girl alone had been. She thought the useless wanderer I had met was her father and he had lived with us in this farmhouse for a little while, but he was an angry man, and when his anger started to come out on Lis; I had made him leave. It has been just the two of us ever since. She was the most important person in my life. My human life. She had turned out magnificent though. She didn't have any fears like I did. She was a strong, smart, and kind human. I knew she was different, but I hadn't wanted to think about it. So, I raised her as human as I could. I met Apollo in the grocery store. He smelled us out and headed straight for us. I tried to turn him away, but he was persistent, and he knew Lis was different. I never thought how different she would be. He never tried to change her, in fact, he doted on her like a father would. A good father. He bought her presents for every birthday, every Christmas even Valentine's Day. She never knew who bought the gifts, they were just there every holiday with her name on them and nothing more. I thought she might question where the money came from to buy the gifts, but she never questioned. I didn't know what I would have told her if she had. And now she wanted to meet him. The new surgeon at the hospital. What would she say if she knew the truth, that I had lied to her for her entire life? Not only was the new surgeon the one who bought all her gifts, but he was my Alpha, I was his Luna and a werewolf, and so was she. She was more though, and Apollo wanted to show her, teach her. I wouldn't have it. She was so young. She hadn't lived yet. She should be going to football games with her friends, sneaking drinks at dances, and finishing her schooling. Meeting regular boys and going out on dates. She needed more time. I would beg for five more years; she could finish some school. Then choose, she still had time. She wasn't close to changing, I would have smelled it on her. She was still my little girl, my human girl. She needed a chance to live and love before her world got turned upside down with all the new rules her lycanthrope family would bring, and she would have to obey. I shuddered at the thought, I had raised her to be an independent thinker, and being a werewolf meant listening to your Alpha.

I would have to talk with Apollo about Gavin, he was getting too pushy. She hadn't chosen a boyfriend, and her first one wouldn't be the Beta. She needed a real human to love first, she needed to know that she had choices. Gavin wouldn't have been my choice for her either, he was too bold, too brassy. Like he owned everything around him, we had a few confrontations over the years and Apollo always settled the matters easily. Gavin should never have entered my home or spoken to Lis; he should have been forbidden to have any contact with her. They all should have been forbidden. She wasn't a part of the pack yet.

I glanced over to the bedside clock; Lis would be just getting out of school. I should get up and shower and start some food. She usually did all the cooking for me but some days I liked to do it. She liked to be responsible in our relationship, and I had encouraged that over the years. One day she would be responsible for more than herself and she needed to be confident she could do it.

I appreciated the air conditioner that Lis insisted I keep running so it cooled my room, I smiled. As a werewolf, I didn't feel the heat or the cold. I was always one temperature, forty-five degrees at all times unless I was hurt, then the temperature soared high. Looking at myself in the dusty cracked mirror, I thought about a shower, but a run would be better. Working nights made me miss running in the fields and rushing up the mountains smelling the cool air and the damp earth. A run would be better, I smiled.

The back door squeaked as I flung it open and started to run along the dusty ground, my bare feet feeling the warmth of the sun-baked soil. I laughed out loud as I took in the scenery. The country air whipped past my snout as I began to change. In seconds I had changed into the wolf that howled to be let out. My strides lengthened and took me further away. The mountains awaited. I howled as I ran calling hello to my pack. Soon there were five of us running together, I in the lead, two white wolves on either side of me, and two brown behind them. We bumped shoulders in playfulness, barking with laughter when one of us lost our footing. We ran awhile and stopped to get water from a mountain stream. It was good to be back among the pack, I missed their company. How would it be if or when Lis made her decision? Would she stay with us or go her own way? I sighed and barked at my friends, nodding my head towards home. I got a few grumbles, but we turned and ran back the way we had come. The night was coming, Lis would be home soon if she weren't already. I was going to cook for her tonight.

I heard the bus long before it turned down our road. The spaghetti sauce was bubbling on the stove and the boiling water was just waiting for the long noodles to be added. I waited another couple of minutes before I added them. The bus stopped at the end of the drive and rumbled on once Lis had got off. I heard her humming as she walked down the gravel driveway. I got up and met her at the screen door. She was tired and looked like she needed to talk.

"Hi bug, how was school?" I asked her as she dropped her heavy book bag in the hallway.

"Water." She mumbled as she walked into the kitchen. I watched her smell the aroma of tomato sauce before she gulped down her cool water. "Mom, how can you be cooking spaghetti in this heat? We could have just had a salad."

"I wanted to feed you today kiddo" I replied. "So, how was school? Did you fail anything?" I grinned as I asked the question. She hadn't failed anything since a first-grade spelling test.

"Nope, no failures today, maybe tomorrow though. I will see what I can do." Lis answered amused.

We chatted about nothing important, but I treasured the conversation we had over dinner. She would be a wonderful leader either in the human world or the lycanthrope one. I wondered which she would choose, I was too afraid to ask.

After dinner we washed the dishes and straightened the kitchen, she helped put together a bit for my lunch making sure it would be a balanced meal. She was so concerned for me, and I appreciated her even more for it.

"I might be a bit late coming home in the morning, Dr. Apollo asked me to fix his schedule, he had to leave for a few days," I mentioned before I left the house.

"A few days, does that mean no BBQ?" Lis asked me.

"I'm not sure honey, I did ask, and he said he would come by but that was before the emergency." I gathered up my things to leave. "I will see if he has left any messages when I get to work. I gotta run now but I will call you before bed. I love you bug, be good, be safe. Do some homework or something will you?" I teased as I kissed her forehead.

"I don't have homework, mom." She sighed. "I finished it on the bus on the way home. I will watch a movie though! With popcorn. See you in the morning, have a good shift. Love you too." She answered as I left the front porch.

The drive to work was uneventful, I watched as the moon rose high in the sky. Another day was done, and she still had no idea. I thanked the goddess for every day that I got to spend with her as a human teenager. Those days were being numbered. I shivered as I thought what she might do. I needed her to understand why I had done what I had. Why I had kept her a secret, I needed her.

CHAPTER SEVEN

Lis

My mom was acting weird. Weirder than she usually was. I knew that she was hiding something. What was it? Was the surgeon a serious boyfriend? Was she afraid to tell me that I would finally have a stepdad? I grimaced at the word as it entered my mind. No that wasn't it. She wasn't any happier than usual and if I were going to have a stepdad, she would be happy. I flicked through the channels on the old television. Nothing appealed to me tonight. I turned it off and grabbed my bowl of popcorn, I would sit on the porch for a minute. The heat had faded with the sun, and I liked to hear the coyotes howl at night. The night sound is silent in the desert except for an occasional cricket chirp. It was too early to go to bed, but I could daydream on the swing. When I thought about the swing my thoughts automatically went to Gavin the god. He was so cute. Way too old for me though. I hadn't even had a boyfriend my age yet. The boys at school seemed so young, so immature. They wouldn't have the sculpted abs of the god that was here yesterday. Was it only one day ago that I had met the stranger, it seemed like I had known him before. Like our souls knew each other. I hadn't been afraid of him more curious than anything. I wondered where he was from, mom had said he worked with her at the hospital so he must live close. I hadn't seen him before, but I didn't go to town much, I preferred the quiet of our house. The squeaking floorboards and faded paint had grown on me.

My bowl of popcorn finished I stood up and checked to make sure the windows were all closed and latched. I went inside and locked the door behind me. I'm not sure why my mom insisted on these precautions, there were no houses nearby, anyone this far out needed a car, and I would hear them drive up. But rules were rules and I listened to all of hers even if they made no sense to me.

I waited until my mom called to say goodnight before I washed the popcorn bowl, turned off all the lights, and went upstairs automatically skipping the one squeaky stair. The house was cooler than last night, but it would still be too hot to sleep, I would stay in Mom's room again. I turned on the air conditioner and then got my pajamas from my room. In minutes I was ready for bed and the air conditioner had cooled the room just enough for me. I lay in bed for a few minutes thinking about school, but my last thoughts were about a green-eyed dark-haired wolf god.

CHAPTER EIGHT
Kadz

I watched as the girl lounged on the swing eating popcorn. She was beautiful there was no doubt. Her long red hair glistened in the moonlight. She would be an even more beautiful lycanthrope. She could be mine. There was no agreement between her and Gavin as of yet. She should have a choice; it was what Apollo was always saying. The humans needed choices. I could go in right now and tell her everything. I would be the one to give her the choices she had. I could be the one to share the rest of her life with. I needed a mate, I was ready, would she be?

She stood up gracefully and checked the windows. She was so ignorant of the beasts outside her house. Not just me but others like me. There had been talk of her since her birth. We knew Rhea had escaped with her; we had killed the father, Warwick, he had been no match for Apollo. Then Apollo had taken to raising Lis, buying her gifts for her birthday. He had been furious when Rhea had torn the tags off and let Lis think she had bought everything. He wanted to be with them, but Rhea had insisted she didn't need them to survive, she wanted to raise Lis to be human. She wanted to lie to her. Hide her other self, her true self. He could help her. Apollo would understand, he knew he was looking for a mate. He had even encouraged it. Apollo had never told them to stay away from Lis, they just had, she was a child. She wasn't any longer though. He watched as she opened the front door and heard the click of the flimsy lock. She thought she was safe. A few minutes later the lights downstairs all extinguished and he heard her climb the old stairs to her room. He heard her turn on the air conditioner and thought it was so unnecessary, she wouldn't need air conditioning if she were a wolf. He imagined her lying beside him ready to laugh and talk over their day. To hold her in his arms for eternity, her red hair cascading over her shoulders those rare beautiful blue eyes looking up at him so trusting. He would care for her if she let him in. He stood and took a step towards the house before he stopped. He was here to watch. That was all. She was ready for him, but he would go slow. Tomorrow, he would officially meet her. With Apollo and Gavin gone and Rhea working nights, he had the daytime free to do whatever he chose. He chose to meet and claim her before Gavin came back. There would be nothing Gavin or Apollo could do if she chose him first.

CHAPTER NINE
Rhea & Apollo

The night shift was quiet. The staff checked on all the patients and did neglected paperwork. Some staff snuck off to get a nap, it happened on nightshift, some staff had families and they kept them awake during the day even if they tried to be quiet. The ones left on the floor talked quietly being mindful of all the residents. Rhea told them she was going to take a quick lunch break and headed to Apollo's office. It smelled like him there, his musky wintery smell. She took out some leftover spaghetti and reheated it in the microwave waiting patiently until the beep announced it was heated through. The vending machine coffee was lukewarm and tasted more like cardboard than coffee. After she finished and tossed the bitter coffee away, she sat in his chair. Absently picking at the worn leather on the arm. Wondering what he had been called away for. She knew most things about him but there was a part of him he kept to himself. There were no family pictures in his office. She knew he had brothers besides Gavin but nothing more than that. For as long as he had been in her life and had been her Alpha, she barely knew him. He was kind and fair, but fierce when he needed to be. His pack looked up to him and rarely challenged any of his choices. She wondered if Warwick would be a different kind of Alpha, then shook her head, it was better not to think of him at all. He had no place in her and Lis's lives. She leaned back and rocked in the leather chair, closing her eyes for a minute.

Rhea? Are you there? She heard Apollo speak to her as her Alpha.

Yes, Apollo, I'm here. Are you okay? She answered quickly.

My brother needs me here for a few days, look after the pack. Gavin and I should be home soon.

Sure, whatever you need. The pack is quiet tonight. Let me know if you need me to do anything while you're gone. You can trust me.

I know Rhea, see you soon. Thanks.

And then he was gone, the connection severed. He hadn't asked me to do anything but straighten up his office. Being Luna wolf to his Alpha was pretty easy, especially in our pack. We were all pretty chill.

I looked through some of his correspondence left on his desk and made a few notes he could look through them when he returned.

I heard the beeping of the various machines helping the patients as they slept fitfully as I walked back to the emergency ward. It was a quiet night. That meant it would be a long night. I smiled at the new girl behind the nursing station desk, whew, she looked to be right out of school. I couldn't even remember her name. I should try harder. I needed to make my human life as important as my pack life or I would get lost in one world. If I were to be lost, I longed for it to be in the human world, but I would never leave Lis to fend for herself in the lycanthrope world. So here I was pretending to be a nurse and pushing my Luna wolf to the back. She howled to be acknowledged. I ignored her.

CHAPTER TEN

Lis

I slept fitfully, tossing and turning. I felt hot even though it was cool in the room. I thought maybe the air conditioner had crapped out, but I could hear it clanking noisily as it spewed cool air into the room. I lay quietly, I didn't hear any noises except the ones made from the old farmhouse. What had awakened me? The room was dark, and I looked at the clock. 1:30 am. It must have just been a dream. I closed my eyes to get back to sleep and I remembered bits of my dream. I had been running through a forest, on a mountain. There was a beautiful stream that splashed down onto rocks and there was an iceberg. How did that get there? I saw a large man who had hair like a rainbow, he was tall enough to touch the stars above his head. He wore leather moccasins, like the Aboriginal people. I had never seen him before then he turned to look at me, like he knew I was watching him. But it was just a dream. Then I saw Gavin and the dark-haired wolf beside him. I shivered as I remembered the black wolf bearing his teeth and taking a step towards me. That is what had woken me up. Why would I be dreaming of wolves, there were coyotes around, but I had never seen any wolves. I blinked my eyes and resolved to get to sleep. I had to stop thinking of Gavin, he was an ass. Too arrogant to be thought of.

I closed my eyes and the next thing I knew my alarm was going off. I felt like I had only a minute of sleep, but it had been hours since I had woken from my dream. Today was going to be a long one. I sighed as I got up and went to shower. I noticed dirt under my fingernails. How had that gotten there? I was sure I had washed before I went to sleep the night before. I had even eaten popcorn and my nails had been clean then. Weird.

Hurriedly I cleaned up and shut off the shower. My mom would be home soon, and I should get some breakfast started for her. Only a couple more shifts and she would be home for a few nights before her day shifts began. I should make sure she asked for days off for my graduation. There was a lot to get organized for the big day. Of course, my birthday would come first but that was just another day. I really should get started on that Valedictorian speech. I should also get my essay ready to be sent to the universities. I had no idea where I should go or what I wanted to pursue, I needed to get some things settled or I would soon be without any education choices. I knew I could get into Brown; the guidance counselor had been steering me in that direction, but I wanted all the choices. I would look up some of the universities and check out the cost of each including the cost of living. I wouldn't set my sites on anything we couldn't afford. My mom would tell me to just pick anything I wanted and to just go for it, but I couldn't let her put us in debt so far that we wouldn't get out for years. It was so unreasonable to spend so much for an education.

Especially since I hadn't decided on a career. Nursing would be easy; my mom could help with everything. I could most likely get a job in the same hospital as her too. I knew I was being unreasonable; I would need my own space eventually. I would have to move out and learn to live without her. I briefly wondered how she would live without me.

I wandered down the stairs as I heard her turn the lock on the front door.

CHAPTER ELEVEN
Katz & Lis

She looked tired. Did she know she had run last night? She had been beautiful; her long red hair had streamed behind her. Taller than most she-wolves she had covered the distance to the forest behind her house in seconds. Her long legs stretched out and her wolf call had been light and happy. She had been free.

She found her friends outside of her bus and they walked towards the small school building. I watched the sway of her hips in her knee-length yellow skirt, the white lacy tank top enclosed her hips, and her red hair seemed brighter against it. She stopped and turned to look around and in seconds her blue eyes collided with mine. I tipped my head in greeting letting her know I had been watching her. She whipped her head back around and raced to catch up to her friends who had waited by the steps for her. When she got to the school doors, I saw her turn quickly to see if I still watched her. Then she turned and entered the school. I would be here when she finished. It was time to introduce myself properly.

I wandered around the small town; I went for a cool drink at the restaurant where Bessie introduced herself. She had questions. A lot of them, mostly who I was and why I was in their small town. Chipper is what I would call her. She told me all about the history and of the families who lived there. How their small town thrived with the finding of gold and silver in the mines. I told her I was a paramedic, new to the town. There was a new ambulance coming in and the hospital had asked for resumes about a month ago. I was here to have my interview with the hospital's HR department. Bessie was a town gossip, and I knew she would have all the local ladies knowing who I was by dinnertime. I would find my mate here. If not Lis, then one of the others.

The lunch bell sounded at the school where Lis was, I strolled over that way. I saw her and her two friends from this morning, walking the perimeter of the schoolyard. They passed through the bleachers that surrounded the football field. The boy walking between them was telling a story with hand gestures, they were laughing. She was beautiful.

Like she could feel my gaze on her she looked up at me. She just stared into my eyes like she could see my soul. I watched her friends quiet as they noticed she wasn't listening to them anymore. As I walked towards the group the other two turned their heads to see who Lis was staring at. I tore my eyes from hers to acknowledge the others.

"Hello, my name is Katz. I'm new in town. I am looking for the hospital. Would you know where it is?" I asked them in my most sincere voice.

"Oh, hey, ya it's not far, Lis's mom works there." The boy said. "Hi Katz, I'm Gabe and this is Madi and Lis." He gestured towards the two girls.

"Hello, Madi and Lis," Kadz drawled the introduction.

He waited for her to speak, he watched her lick her lips, the wet making her lips shimmer in the heat.

"Hi Katz. That's a different name." She answered in her melodic voice. Like an angel. "The hospital is a couple blocks up the street. Only about a ten-minute walk. Are you hurt? Do you need a ride up there?"

"No, I'm fine and I can walk. It's for an interview. I hope to be the new paramedic in town."

"Well, it's just that way, there should be signs to follow once you get to the main street. Good luck with your interview."

I could listen to her speak all day. It was like a symphony of angelic voices coming from her. Did she know?

"Thank you, Lis, for your help. Nice to meet you all. See you around town I hope." I thanked them as I turned towards the road. I looked back and saw her watching me. That was a start.

CHAPTER TWELVE

Gavin

I had to leave. Tyler's mountain and I had seen enough of each other. I needed to get back to Lis. I liked Tyler the most of all my brothers, but I would never tell him that.

Apollo was fair and tried to teach me stuff, but he was just too overbearing. He treated me like I was a youngster, not the god that I was. I needed my own pack, world, realm, whatever it was, I needed my own life. I was tired of following him around like a lost puppy. The secret growing garden had been so eye-opening. I knew I would be able to find it again, Apollo said it moved but it was always on Tyler's mountain. Tyler had given me the secret and said not to share it with anyone. He finally trusted me with one of his secrets. He said he understood my need to learn and to grow. He understood that I needed my own space. I couldn't live on the mountain with him, but I could visit anytime. I told him about Lis and that she would be my mate, forever. Tyler had understood that completely. He had fallen in love with a human, well she was a witch, but she didn't know she would be staying on his mountain yet. He was so sure of himself. I hoped he would be happy with the human witch. She seemed like a lot of trouble for a human. She was so naïve. Then again so was Lis but in a separate way. Lis was born to be a werewolf, she was born to run with him, to lead with him. He just needed her mother, to give her a little push in the right direction. Kadz knew she was ready; he could sniff it. I had to get back before he did something that couldn't be reversed.

Finally, Apollo had said his goodbyes to the group on the mountain. I smirked at Tyler as I watched the human girl, Ava, hold onto his hand. She looked a little stunned, must be the electric current running through her at Tyler's touch. The little group had saved the world from being flooded. Good for them, I had a werewolf to get back to. She would be waiting for me; she just didn't know it yet.

Once we reached the treeline Apollo and I changed to wolf form and howled as we ran down the mountain. Our home awaited. The trees blurred by as we pounced through the air. At this rate, we would be home within hours. I ran faster than I ever had before, I was still a step behind Apollo. Would I ever match him in speed and strength? I hoped so, I needed to if I was going to be my own Alpha.

In my mind, I pictured Lis with her little red dress on and her long red locks trailing down her back. In wolf form, she would be the perfect color against my black. That was it Ian had found his mate with Enid, Tyler had found Ava, Apollo had Rhea, it was my turn to find my mate. Lis was it! I just had to get home and tell her what she was, what I was, and that she didn't really have a choice, she would be my mate.

I stumbled a moment as I looked through Lis's sight, what the hell was Kadz doing talking with her and her friends, and why the hell was she staring at him as he walked away?

I needed to get home.

CHAPTER THIRTEEN
Rhea

Rhea, wake up. I need to speak to you, now. I heard the internal wolf message and turned over. It was too early to get up. *She's ready Rhea. Are you awake?*

What? What does he mean by *She's ready*?

Apollo, where are you? I'm awake now. Give me a few minutes to grab some caffeine.

I could tell by the sunlight coming in the faded curtains it was early in the day. Lis would still be at school for a few hours. I stretched and moaned a little bit. I would sleep tonight if it wasn't busy at the hospital. Coffee. Not the decaffeinated kind either.

Finding some running clothes, I wiped the sleep from my eyes before I fully opened them. Slipped on my runners and bounced down the stairs anxious for my first cup of coffee. The house was so quiet. I liked it that way and so did Lis.

We were independent females. I hoped she would choose her human life.

The coffee was ready in minutes. It was so hot, and I drank it like it was a cool glass of water. Delicious.

I'm ready. Where are you, Apollo? I sipped on a second cup while I patiently waited for his reply. He really was good to us. I'm not sure where we would have ended up if he hadn't stepped in when he had. I just wanted him to quit pushing me to tell Lis. She didn't need to know at least not yet.

Meet me in the woods. Five minutes. The pack will be there in ten. Apollo's voice entered my mind.

Okay, see you in five. I answered back quickly. I tossed back the warm coffee and placed the empty cup on the counter.

Making sure my hair was in place, I didn't like the unkempt look some of the other werewolves favored. I went out the back door and smiled as I started running. This part of the Lycanthrope world I loved. The freedom. I could run for miles and never get tired. I made it to our meeting spot on the ledge of the small mountains that surrounded our town in under five minutes. Apollo would not like it if I were late.

I groomed a minute before I heard his paws pounding the dirt on the mountain. Then I heard a second pair. Gavin. I still had to speak to him about Lis. I needed to make them understand that Lis was human first, not last.

In seconds they emerged from the trees. He was so bold, so authoritative. I had loved him from the minute I met him, but Lis would always come first. He had settled for being in the shadows of our lives, but I knew it wouldn't be for much longer. I knew he had always been there for Lis, for the moment when she changed, I just happened to be her mom, so he let me stay. I had kept them apart so she would understand that I was her mom, and I was important too. Lis didn't need to follow Apollo because he was her Alpha, she could choose to be human. I feared every day that I would lose her to Apollo and Gavin. That she would leave me behind. She was the born leader of them. We didn't know how that happened, but it was a fact. She should have changed long ago but she hadn't and for that, I had been grateful. I would keep every second I had with her as a human that I could.

Thanks for being here Rhea, Apollo's gruff voice entered my mind. *I missed you the last couple of days. We will have to go back for a wedding soon. Tyler asked Ava to marry him.*

I smiled and pushed my snout into his neck, I had missed him also. *Hi there. You smell nice. If you want, I can go with you to the wedding, or I can watch the pack, whatever you need.*

He nuzzled me back before we heard a gagging noise beside him.

Is this a pack meeting or a make-out session? If it's the second I will just head back down the mountain. Gavin mumbled.

Gavin. Apollo growled. *Greet the pack as they come up, would you?* And he bumped his shoulder to push him back towards the clearing.

Whatever you need Apollo. Gavin echoed my earlier comment.

We watched him stroll over to the landing and welcome the first member of our pack.

Rhea, Apollo started, *Lis is ready to change. Gavin and Kadz have both smelled it coming. Do you want it to happen without her knowing it? I know you want her to stay human, but she can't. She won't. If she changes now, she will have time to decide where to go to school. Somewhere that she can be close by if she needs us. Plus, Gavin has mentioned that she dream changed. She thought she was human, but she showed up as a werewolf. Just coming home Gavin said Kadz met her and her friends at school today. He has made contact, and he is looking for a mate.*

Katz? I questioned; *Lis told me she met Gavin the other day when he showed up unannounced at my house Apollo. He was supposed to stay away from her. You said you would take care of it. She isn't ready. I would have smelled her change as well. She's just a regular brilliant teenager, a human one.*

I spoke to Gavin and that is why we left together; I didn't realize that Katz was meeting her as well. Maybe we need to examine our roles here in this community Rhea. Our pack needs us, and we are spending too much time as humans here. The jobs are too demanding right now. We need to prioritize. We will be talking to Lis, today. Rhea, I am insisting we do this. It's the best thing for her and for the pack. Apollo waited for my response.

I suppose letting Lis know would give her a chance to decide what she wanted. She could still go to school with some help from us. I was kind of curious to see her werewolf form. She would be beautiful. I still didn't want her near Gavin or Katz for that matter. I would have to tell her. Tonight. I just hoped she could forgive me for deceiving her for so long.

I will talk to her tonight, Apollo, I answered him quietly, *I still don't want her to be mated to either of them though. She is too young. She can hardly make up her mind about which university to attend I do not want her making a life choice for a mate. Not yet Apollo. Please give her time to adjust to one life-altering choice at a time.*

Rhea, you've raised a brilliant, beautiful, forgiving daughter. She will know you meant only the best for her. Apollo said as he nuzzled my cheek. *She won't have much time to choose a mate, but I will let the boys know it is her choice and they will have to abide by it.*

Thank you. I whispered into his ear.

Let's get things sorted with the pack. Apollo said as he turned toward the pack who were waiting patiently for him to acknowledge them and start the meeting. We stood side by side like we had for years. We were one, him and I.

Tonight, I would tell my daughter that for the last seventeen years, I had lied about her birth and her father. I would tell her she had a choice to make. She could turn her back on the lycanthrope community and me or she could embrace her new self and learn to change.

A tear fell from my eye as I looked out at my pack, they would fight to the end for me and I for them. How would Lis feel when she found out that she had a whole family waiting to meet her and teach her?

I shivered and blinked. No more tears. She was a fighter, she was strong, and she would handle it.

She had no choice but to.

CHAPTER FOURTEEN

Lis And The Pack

What a weird day. I had been feeling sluggish and quite cranky. Madi and I argued after meeting Katz during lunch. She said he was weird, I told her not to be so childish. He was good-looking. He seemed different but that was just because she was used to all the people she had grown up with in this town. I wasn't sure what made me say it, but I told her she shouldn't be jealous because he had looked at me rather than her. I knew she was always the center of attention, and she liked it. That's what made her a great cheerleader. She was also really friendly, and I don't know what it was that she didn't like about Katz. Then she got even madder when Gabe took my side. He had actually put his arm around my shoulders when he defended me. I shrugged him off, but she said we belonged together, and if she was going to be a third wheel she would hang out with other people and leave us alone. We didn't speak for the rest of the day, and I went home on the bus without talking to either of them, even though Gabe tried to talk with me. Was it just me? Had I been too mean to her? Why did I even accuse her of being jealous? I didn't even know the new guy in town.

When I got home my mom wasn't there and she hadn't left a note or anything. The car was in the driveway so she must have just gone for a run before dinner. The one day that I needed a talk, and she wasn't there. I was so hot. I had a quick tepid shower, changed into loose clothes, and went onto the deck to swing in my chair. I took out an English book and dived into my homework. I had been so cranky at school I didn't even do my work. I knew I needed to finish it as every grade would count towards my GPA and that's what the universities looked at first. I was so tired I barely read two pages before my eyes dropped close. In minutes I was sound asleep.

I woke when my mom touched my shoulder.

"Hey sleepyhead, time to get up." She nudged me softly.

"Hey Mom, how was your run?" I questioned her as I noticed her running gear.

"It was great. How was your day? Did you fail anything today?" she teased me as I sat up slowly.

"Just my friendship," I answered.

"Hey, what happened? Madi is forgiving, was it, Gabe? Did you break his fragile heart?" she lightly asked.

"Mom, no, it was a real fight this time. I was totally a bitch. I should call Madi. I wish we had never met that Katz guy. He is just trouble." I sat up and got comfortable then told her everything that had happened and what I had said. I told her Gabe was in love with me and Madi and she was just too stubborn to acknowledge him and his feelings. He shouldn't have put me in between them either.

"So, you met Katz?" my mom asked, "What did you think of him?"

"Mom, I probably won't see him again. I think he was just passing through. If he doesn't get the job as the new paramedic, he will leave. There's nothing in this town to keep him here. I need to call Madi. Could we just have a quick salad for supper? It's too hot to heat the house and I'm really tired. I must be getting a flu bug." I made a move to stand up, but my mom caught my arm.

"Sit down a moment Lis. We need to have a serious conversation."

"Are you okay?" I asked her.

"Of course, I'm fine." She replied. "I don't know where to start."

"At the beginning Mom. Are you sure you're, okay? You look kind of green."

"Okay, the beginning. Remember when I told you that your dad was not important? That he didn't deserve to be with us?"

"My dad? What does he have to do with this? Is he here? Does he want to come back? You can't let him. He was abusive Mom, to you and me."

"Lis." she interrupted my diatribe "No he isn't back. I would never let him near you. But I need to tell you about him. He wasn't all human."

"I know Mom, he was a monster. Any man who hits women is a monster."

"Hmmm, I agree Lis, but he wasn't just that. The man who you think was your father isn't. He was just the man who helped us to hide from your real father. Your real father was a lycanthrope, a werewolf. He was an Alpha, and his name was Warwick."

"My real father. A werewolf. Come on Mom, I'm not a child who has illusions about her real dad, and there are no such things as werewolves. Why tell me we need to have a serious conversation and then tell me this?" I tried to stand again but my Mom's arm shot out and held me in place.

"You need to listen Lis. I only have a brief time to tell you. After that, it is out of my hands. Werewolves are real. I am one and so are you. I am a Luna wolf to Apollo. I have been since you were little. Apollo is my Alpha, my pack leader. Gavin is my side mate, the Beta to Apollo, his brother. Apollo is the same person as Dr. Apollo, the surgeon, at the hospital. I have known him for years. I have loved him for years. I wanted to keep you out of this life, wanted to keep you human and in the shadows for as long as I could. Lis, you're growing up, and you are going to change. You were born a lycanthrope. You are a werewolf too."

I blinked as I looked at her in silence. "I'm a werewolf?" I questioned before I turned my head and threw up over the side of the leaning porch.

"Lis!" I heard my Mom exclaim. "Lis, it's going to be okay, I won't leave you."

Alissa. Lis. I'm Apollo. You're going to be okay. Trust your mom to take care of you. I screamed out loud as I heard the rumbling deep voice inside my head.

"Mom? Who is in my head? Am I going insane?"

"It's Apollo, it's how we communicate Lis. He can speak to all the pack like that. Even when he is in human form. I can too."

Gently my mom sat me back down. I was shaking. I was a werewolf. My real dad was an Alpha. My mom had a boyfriend/Alpha. I had to take these facts in and ask the right questions. I was a hairy werewolf.

"Mom?" I questioned "Do you eat people? Are we monsters? Am I going to eat people?" my voice raised and shook on the last word.

"No Lis, we aren't monsters. We eat meat, but not human meat. I prefer the grass and berries. We can live off of human food too. Fast food is no good though. We are not monsters. There are hundreds of werewolves around the world each with their own Alpha. I don't know where your real father is, nor do I care. It's still just you and me. Okay?" my mom answered softly.

"Ahem." came a deep voice from the front porch stairs.

My mom and I both looked up.

Apollo was there, I knew it was him even before he spoke.

"Hello Lis. You will not be alone ever again. We are your family. Even in human form. We look out for one another."

He was intimidating. He was tall and perfect in every way. He was the perfect match for my mom's tiny stature. I watched as she lowered her eyes once then bobbed her head down and up in deference to his rank. I knew my breath hitched as I saw on either side of him his Beta wolf, Gavin, and the dark-eyed paramedic Kadz, and behind them were others. I had seen them all in my dream, they looked just like the wolves that they were. No, I corrected myself not wolves, werewolves.

In silence, I stood up and looked at them all. Then I turned and jumped off the porch and started running. I had to go. I couldn't hear anymore.

I heard my mom as she yelled at me to come back, I heard Apollo tell her to let me be.

I heard growling behind me and started to turn, just in time I saw Gavin and Katz bump shoulders as they ran behind me, Gavin snarled and bit at Katz. They acted like wolves, but they were human and ran on two legs.

"Lis, you need to stop. You haven't even changed yet; you're going to tire out and then I will have to carry you all the way back." The green-eyed Gavin said.

"Run Lis, get it out. I will follow you until you're ready to go home. I will gladly carry you back." The dark-eyed Katz replied.

I slowed down and caught my breath. "Go away, both of you. You're both liars."

I sank to the dry ground and cried silent tears.

"Get away from her. Both of you. You have no right to be here. Neither of you. Go now." I heard my mom say. She sounded different. Authoritative.

I heard the two males leave.

"Lis? I know it's a lot to take in. I will always be here, come on let's go back home. You can ask me anything you want." My mom cradled my shoulders and let me cry.

"Mom?" I whispered.

"Yes bug?" she replied quietly.

"I don't want to be a werewolf."

"Let's get back to the house. Have a sleep and talk about this tomorrow alright?"

I let her stand me up and together we walked silently back to the house. The others were all gone. Mom made a hot cup of cocoa and handed it to me. I hadn't realized I was shivering.

"Come on Lis, let's go to bed, we can talk in the morning."

I slowly climbed the stairs, too tired to hear the squeaking of the second stair. Once I reached her room I stopped. I couldn't go in there with her. Without glancing back, I went to my room and closed the door. I heard my mom catch her breath, but she let me go. For hours I lay in bed fully clothed shivering under my blanket. I watched the shadows on the ceiling first through the dark then lighten as a new day approached.

I was a werewolf. What did that mean?

CHAPTER FIFTEEN
Gavin & Kadz

"You scared her. She should have been left alone. What both of you did was wrong. Now I need you both to look out for her, nothing more. Like her big brothers. Keep the pack from crowding her, let her come into her she-wolf on her own. Keep her from harming herself and others. We are not rabid dogs we are werewolves. Remind her of the family she was born into. She was born for more than either of you wants her for. She is off limits." Apollo's voice rumbled out the last sentence in his Alpha tone. It was unquestionable.

Kadz and I walked out of the house that we shared, quietly going over each word Apollo had said. There had to be a loophole. For once we walked in silence. Each of us thought about how to get closer to Lis while keeping our distance. We had to look out for her, like brothers. Kadz should have just left it at that, there were other females he could choose to mate with. He had to know that Lis was meant for me.

"Hey Kadz," I turned to him, "how about you let me help Lis with her transitions and you go south to look for a mate. There are a lot of she-wolves there. Lis is an innocent. She isn't ready to settle down with a life mate. She doesn't need both of us to watch over her."

"Nice try Gavin. I met her first, she can choose. One as a brother the other as a mate."

"You think you met her first? I met her days ago at her house. Lis dream changed to find me. She will be my mate. I will always look out for her Kadz. I will win."

"You won't win. She will choose me. She feels comfortable with me already. See you around. Brother."

I watched as Kadz walked away, his gait smooth and even, like all werewolves. Lis wouldn't choose him. She belonged to me. I was a God, and I could make her come to me. But did I want to do that? I was beginning to understand the reasoning behind why Apollo said that humans have choices, and we are just there to guide them to those. Would she choose Kadz, or would she choose me?

I had to figure out something to tip the scales a little in my favor. Turning away from the direction Kadz was walking I hurried my step and headed back to Rhea's house. If I was going to get Lis to trust me, I had to speak to her mom first.

CHAPTER SIXTEEN

Rhea & Lis

I barely slept, tossing and turning all night. What would I say? How would she react? What would she choose? How would I let her go? Dam those boys for interfering with our lives.

Finally, as the sun rose and made the dingy white walls brighter, I pulled myself out of bed and headed for the shower. I had to get this day over with. Now that Lis knew about me and herself, I had to tell her everything. Even though she wasn't a she-wolf yet. The pack would be waiting to meet her. I shivered as I thought about it. She was growing and leaving me sooner than I wanted her to.

I stared at the ceiling; pictures of grotesque wolves danced among the shadows. I was a werewolf. A hairy, monster. Would I change when a full moon came? Would it hurt? Didn't I have any choice in the matter? I had been attracted to the dangerous Kadz; he was the black werewolf. Gavin the God with those abs and those jeans, was also a werewolf, he was the green-eyed black-haired werewolf. My mom was also a wolf, I bet she would be just as pretty in wolf form as she was in human form. Apollo, the surgeon/Alpha, my Alpha. He looked scary; he hadn't seemed gentle at all. His piercing eyes looked like they saw everything at once and he could probably read my mind. Or something like that. Would he know everything I did and said now? I needed to figure this out. I still had months of school left. I hadn't even got a prom date lined up. My Valedictorian speech was still in pieces. I wasn't even eighteen. I needed to speak to my mom. I waited until the sun was up and slowly made my way downstairs.

My mom was sitting at the kitchen table with her coffee and a paper and pen. I knew what that meant. We were going to do a list. A pros and cons list. It was what we had done to figure out all the major changes we had had while I was growing up.

"Mom?" my voice cracked.

She was up and wrapped me in her arms before I could say another word. I broke down and cried until I couldn't anymore.

"It's going to be okay Lis; you were born for this. I'm so sorry that I didn't tell you before. I just wanted you to stay you, without all the responsibilities of pack life. I wanted you to be human. I know now I shouldn't have kept it all from you, I was just thinking of myself, I am so sorry Lis, so deeply sorry. Please don't be mad at me, ask me anything you want. I will answer anything."

We sat down at the old, scarred table and talked, all day. We used up a roll of toilet paper wiping our eyes and blowing our noses. We cried some more; we laughed a little bit. She was still my mom. I was still her human little girl. At least until I changed. We didn't know when that would be, but she would be there to help me through it when the time came.

Just before dinner time, we heard a knock on the front door. I watched my mom as her eyes turned the yellow of her wolf and she straightened up as she growled. I would need to get used to that. I wondered what my growl would sound like.

"Hello Rhea, It's just me. Can I come in?"

Before she could answer, Gavin came strolling in and went straight to the cupboard, grabbed a tall glass, and helped himself to some iced tea from the fridge.

"Gavin? What are you doing here? Apollo said to give Lis some room." My mom asked him in a tight voice.

"Relax Rhea, I'm here to see how Lis is doing. If she has any questions, she would like to ask but is too scared to ask you, her mom." He turned his head towards me next.

"Hello, Lis. Are you doing okay today?" His silken voice soothed my nerves just a little bit. "If you need anything just ask. You are a part of the pack family; we have no secrets. It won't be just you two anymore. That might be scary for you but if you think about it a bit you will see that a larger family is fantastic. You have a large family of siblings now. You will always have a place to sleep should you need it. We all run at various times so you can choose your running mates. The mountains that surround us are abundant with wildlife and flora, you will never be hungry again. The lycanthrope family is active throughout the entire world. If you need anything you can just ask."

"Hi, Gavin. My mom and I have talked all day. I do have one question. Can you show me how you change?"

I heard my mom gasp inwardly. I looked at her and saw her fear. Did that look mean that it would hurt?

"Yeah, I can show you. It's okay Rhea, I got Apollos back off message loud and clear. Lis will be safe with me. I won't let anything happen to her. Come on, let's go for a little run. It helps relax me and it should help you too." He held out his hand.

I looked over at my mom, she had been quietly listening to our exchange. I looked back to Gavin and put my hand in his, I jolted at the electric current that went through my body. I heard his low growl of approval and looked up. His eyes were pure green ice. I felt more than heard his werewolf howl in acceptance. This was nice.

"We won't be home till dark, Rhea. Don't worry. She's safer with me than anywhere else. I promise." Gavin assured my mom as we walked to the front doors.

"Be safe Lis and listen to Gavin. He will take care of you." My mom said as we hugged.

"You should take your shoes off Lis; you will get used to being barefoot and it will be easier to change without them on your feet." I looked down at my runners, we had saved for two months to buy them. I had always carefully looked after all my clothing. Without hesitating, I unlaced my shoes and placed them on the porch stairs.

"Okay, I'm ready. Let's go see how this is done. Bye, mom. See you soon." I blew her a kiss as Gavin, and I started a slow jog. In minutes we were flat-out running.

We ran faster than I ever had, I wasn't even winded. I laughed as my hair whipped around my shoulders. All too soon, we entered the forested area, and I looked over at Gavin. He wasn't his human self anymore but a beautiful green-eyed wolf. I didn't even hear him change. It couldn't have been that bad if he had done it so easily. Together we darted through the trees, and he gave a loud bark as we came to a picturesque clearing. There was a watering hole, large boulders piled on one side and trees surrounded the other sides. It was just like I had seen in my dream. The ledge of the mountain and all the rocks jutting out where the pack had been. I bent down by the water's edge and grabbed a handful of water. I could see my cheeks were flushed by the run, but my eyes were what caught my attention. They were bright yellow. Not my eyes but my werewolf eyes. We were one yet it seemed like she had a mind of her own. In seconds I looked at the other set of eyes which watched mine. Those piercing green eyes met my yellow ones and he bumped my shoulder. I looked back at the water and saw that my eyes were normal once again. My wolf decided not to emerge just yet.

We spent the evening talking. I felt like he still kept secrets from me. He was the person I needed. He was like the big brother I never had. He kept his distance; he didn't touch me again, so I wondered if I had felt the electricity between us at all. He was funny and told me stories of the pack. I learned all their names and I asked about the dream I had had the week before. He told me I had already changed but in dream form not in human form. He said my she-wolf was looking for her pack and wouldn't show herself until she felt safe enough to.

Gavin explained what he knew of my parentage. He had known my father. That is all he would tell me about that. He told me of Apollo and how he had taken an interest in me and that he and my mom had been together for about fifteen years. My mom had boyfriends but that was to keep her cover and hide us from my father. Once Apollo had made my mom his Luna, she hadn't had another mate. I was glad he explained that to me. I wouldn't have to worry about her so much while I was away at university now. Oh, I had forgotten about school. I realized that I missed a school day today. When I told Gavin he actually laughed.

I was upset, I had a perfect attendance record. It looked good on the applications. It showed that I was dependable and took my education seriously.

He told me that I would have plenty of time for schooling if I wanted to pursue that avenue. I would live longer than my human counterpart. If I chose lycanthrope life. He explained that while everyone had been waiting for me to grow up, change, and lead. I did have the final choice. If I wanted to be human, I could be. Did I want that? I had just found out about my werewolf personality. What would she like to do, to be, could I just turn my back on her and continue with my human life? I suppose I had a choice to make. Human or werewolf.

I thought about that for the rest of the evening. Gavin and I ran the mountainside and we talked. He was truly knowledgeable, and he treated me well. Apollo would be happy to hear that.

We finally made our way back to the house. It was quiet, the moon had risen. It should have made seeing harder, but it didn't. When I asked Gavin about it, he said my wolf saw better in the dark than in the daylight. That's when our human eyes were better.

My mom was on the porch waiting for us when we got there.

"Hey. How are you doing Bug?" She asked me before I could answer.

"I'm good mom. Gavin was genuinely nice. He didn't show me how to change but explained that my wolf would decide when she was ready to emerge. I did see her though. In the water. She has yellow eyes."

"I have a feeling Lis will be fine Rhea. She is strong and smart; her heart will guide her."

I looked over at Gavin in gratitude. I reached out to hug him and he sidestepped just staying out of arms reach. I thought our day together had bonded us, maybe I was wrong.

"Come on Lis, I made a bite to eat. You should get inside and clean up. You're not going to miss another day of school, okay?" My mom opened the door for me to enter.

"Okay. See ya, Gavin. Thanks for today. I needed it. I have a much clearer head now than I did yesterday." I paused a moment, unsure if I should ask the next question. "Will I see you tomorrow?" I asked anyway.

"I'm busy in the morning but if you need me, I can be around. Whatever you need Lis." He replied as I stepped over the threshold to my home. "Whatever you need." I heard him softly repeat as I closed the door.

My heartbeat loudly. What did he mean by that? Why had he deflected my hug? As I thought back on our evening, I realized he hadn't touched me since his wolf had bumped my shoulder. He hadn't touched me as a human since he had shown up and electrified me when I held his hand. What if what I needed was him? Would he still be so giving if I asked for that? I wondered.

I sat down and ate the pasta my mom had made without tasting a bite of it. Thoughts swirled in my head of the last twenty-four hours. I would be okay. I hadn't thought of school or the valedictorian speech or of homework at all. I was a lycanthrope, which felt more real to me than anything else ever had. Once my shock had subsided, I realized that I was ready. I had a family ready to meet me. I had an Alpha who knew me and had stayed by me to oversee my human life until I was ready to embrace my Lycanthrope family. I wouldn't disappoint them.

I showered and shampooed my hair until it gleamed. It smelled like coconut.

Finally, I found my bedroom and closed the door. I had come up with a plan and I would have a full day tomorrow. I climbed into bed, shut off the little lamp at my bedside, and slept soundly through the night. Unhindered by any dreams.

CHAPTER SEVENTEEN

Lis & Kadz

Renewed with a sense of purpose I bounced out of bed as the alarm sounded. Today I said my goodbyes to my old life. I had chosen to be a werewolf.

I washed my face and brushed my hair until it glistened in the sunlight. I was extra careful applying my minimal makeup. I dressed in my best outfit. A dark blue cap sleeve shirt and grey capris. I pulled my hair back into a long ponytail and held it in place with a dark blue scrunchie. I looked in my closet for the blue-heeled sandals I kept for special occasions.

"Wow, you look nice, extra nice today." My mom commented as I entered the kitchen for a quick bite before I left for school.

"Today is important. I've decided to embrace my new family, my lycanthrope family. I also have to apologize to Madi and Gabe for blowing them off. They are my family too. They need to know about this. It's major Mom and they should know it."

"Honey," my mom started, "You can't tell them. It's forbidden. If the humans know about us, it would change everything."

"Mom!" I cried, "They have to know, they're my best friends. I can't just abandon them after all our years of friendship!"

"Lis, honey. Friendships end all the time, for many reasons. They will move on and find other friendships, especially as they head into university. I'm not saying you should end your friendships, but you have to keep our secret. Can you do that?" my mom placed her hand on my arm in comfort.

"Well, I haven't changed so technically I am not a lycanthrope yet." Her hand squeezed my arm gently.

"Lis, it's important."

"Fine Mom, I won't spill the beans." I harumphed

"Thanks. Now, what are you having for breakfast?" she smiled.

"Toast would be fine. I'm not that hungry." I looked up at my mom, she looked different today. Younger. Did she dye her hair? "Mom? You look different today. Did you dye your hair? Get a new outfit? Are you on days off from the hospital?"

"I am on extended holidays from work. I asked for a few days and explained we had some family issues we needed to work on and then I asked for my holidays to coincide with that. So as of yesterday,

I am all yours until your graduation. I won't leave you when you change Lis. You are my main priority. You always have been."

"Oh, wow Mom that's awesome! Could we travel somewhere we haven't been? I mean when I'm not at school. I can't miss any more days, or I will lose my attendance record."

"We can talk about it tonight when you get home from school. I have to run into town for some supplies, but I should be back for dinner."

"Okay, I gotta get going. See you later. Love you." I grabbed my bag and kissed my mom on the cheek.

"Bye bug, have a wonderful day. See you later." She echoed.

As I sat on the bus, I thought about how my conversation would change. I had to tell Madi and Gabe. How could I do it without telling them? They were both brilliant, but down to earth. Would they even believe that lycanthropes existed?

I watched the town grow bigger as we approached and saw the shopkeepers outside their businesses sweeping the front steps and sidewalks. The red patio umbrellas at the café were closed the lights turned off still. A new day to get ready for. The brick building of the school soon appeared. It was quite big for our town; we had a lot of kids from around the outer communities come here. The schools there only went to sixth grade. I smiled when I saw Madi and Gabe standing next to each other. I guess she had forgiven him for taking my side in our fight. Was it just two days ago? So much had happened in the last forty-eight hours. I had to tell them.

The brakes on the bus squealed to a stop in its usual space and I bounced up. I almost ran off the bus to get to them.

"Madi, I'm sorry I was such an ass."

"Lis, I'm sorry I was such a jerk."

We laughed as we spoke at the same time. We hugged and said no more fighting.

"Hey, do I get a hug too?" Gabe laughed as we jumped on him from either side.

"Okay, enough is enough." He mumbled from under us as we laughed together.

"Is there a reason why you have your nice sandals on today, Lis?" Madi asked as we fixed our hair while we walked towards the front doors.

"I just wanted to look nice. My mom had some time off, so she made breakfast for me. We do need to talk, but it can wait till lunch." I replied.

"Okay, see you guys later," Madi said as she went off to her first class.

"Lis. We should talk too," Gabe said as we headed to our first class.

"I know. Let's just wait a minute longer. I like us as friends Gabe." I softly said.

"You know we could be more than that Lis. You know I want to be."

"Not yet Gabe, please, not yet." I almost begged quietly.

"Okay. Not yet." He said as we found our seats in class.

The rest of the morning went by in a blur. I had missed a few notes from yesterday and I needed to get those caught up. Finally, the lunch bell rang. I was ravenously hungry. Madi and Gabe must have been too, they rested their backs on the lockers beside mine waiting for me.

"I'm so hungry. What do you have for lunch?" I said as I grabbed my lunch from my locker. "Are we going outside? We should."

"Let's go see what we have to switch," Madi said.

For years we had combined our lunches that way we all got what we wanted, and our parents thought we had healthy appetites. It had worked out perfectly.

"Well, that was so good, Gabe your mom makes the best cinnamon buns." Madi moaned as she patted her flat stomach.

"I have been thinking, do you guys believe in lycanthropes?" I just blurted it out.

"Lycanthropes?" Madi questioned.

"Like, werewolves? Humans who change into wolves when the moon is full. That's just movie stuff, Lis." Gabe replied. "There are no such things as werewolves. Wolves, yes. Werewolves, no."

"What class are you taking? I haven't heard of any that ask about werewolves." Madi asked.

"It's not for a class. I was simply curious that's all." I replied. "I believe they are real."

"No way." Gabe reiterated. "Our bodies can't change back and forth. Bones are bones, they can't change. Humans are human and animals are animals."

"What if it was possible? What if humans could change? What if there are lycanthropes right now in our town, our school? Do you think you could tell them apart from the regular people?"

"Well sure, they would be hairy, and their bones would be different. They would probably smell like wet dogs. Their heads would probably be bigger, and they would have to have big noses. Like a snout, and they would only eat meat. Their eyes would be yellow like wolves too." Gabe rattled off every one of my fears.

"Lis, why are you asking?" Madi asked again.

"It was just a thought Madi. I must have had a dream or something and it stuck in my mind. We should get going. The bell is going to ring soon." I started to get up.

I made a squeak as I saw the dark-haired Kadz strolling across the football field.

"You two, go ahead, I'll catch up."

"Lis, we aren't going to leave you out here with an almost stranger," Gabe said.

"It's okay." I thought quickly, "My mom said he was hired, and he just needs to find some friends around here.

"Let's go, Gabe," Madi said. " Lis will be fine, and we don't want to be late." She tugged on his arm.

"Okay, but don't be late Lis." Gabe eyed Kadz as he approached us. He nodded his head at Kadz and looked once more at me before he let Madi turn him away.

"Hi Lis," His voice purred my name, "How are you doing today? Need any help? Have any questions?" His eyes took in my appearance, lingering on my hair and then returning to my eyes.

"Hi Kadz," I replied, I sounded winded like I had just run a marathon. "What are you doing here? My mom said you were supposed to stay away from me. I haven't changed. I still have to finish school. I don't have any questions. Yet."

"You won't be alone Lis. If you need anything, just think of me, of my name and I will hear you. I won't be far away." He turned to walk away and stopped. "Lis you smell like coconut. I like it." He smiled a crooked smile and walked away.

I watched him for a minute, my heart pounding in my chest. He would take control of me if I let him. He would consume me. I couldn't let that happen. Dimly I heard the bell ring signaling the end of lunch. I blinked, shook my head, turned, and raced back to the school. I would think about him later. Right now, I had school to think of.

For the rest of the day, I sat in all my familiar seats surrounded by familiar faces absorbing all the facts presented by the teachers. But all I could think about was the dark-haired dark-eyed wolf who said he liked my coconut shampoo.

CHAPTER EIGHTEEN
Lis-The Change

I tried to talk with Madi between periods, but she was behind on an assignment and had to hurry to class. Gabe was sure there was no such thing as werewolves, so I didn't bother trying to talk with him. I daydreamed about Gavin and Kadz, would all the wolves treat me like they did? Would they accept me into their families so easily? My mom said that I wasn't ready. Would it be so bad to be part of a large family? My mom was already a part of that family. She was the one who had kept me away and had held onto secrets my whole life. What else had she kept from me, I wondered as I stared out the classroom windows. I must have made a sound as I noticed Kadz waiting by the bus stop. What was he doing here?

"Lis? You, okay?" Gabe whispered.

"Oh, ya, must have dozed off," I replied with a smile in his direction. "Actually, I don't feel well, just a little tired," I said as I raised my hand. I had to get out of here. I had an urgent need to get to Kadz.

With the permission of the teacher, I gathered my stuff and headed to my locker. My hands shook as I dialed the combination. I had to try twice before I finally opened the flimsy metal lock. I had to get out. The walls were closing in on me. I needed fresh air.

Finally, after a few tense minutes, I ran to the doors that enclosed me inside the stifling building. I heard the door slam open and felt the cool air of the outside touch my heated face. I bent over as I gathered in deep breaths.

I'm here, you're not alone Lis.

I gasped as I heard his voice tumble through my heated brain.

"Where are you?" I breathed out loud.

Open your eyes, Lis, I'm right here.

I took a breath, stood upright and opened my eyes. The light was so bright. He was there. He wouldn't leave me.

Come, love, let's run. You need it.

We took off at a breathtaking pace. If anyone saw us, they would have only seen two blurry figures running across the fields. I felt better as the cool air rushed over my heated cheeks. We ran as far and as fast as I could. Eventually, we ended up in the forest among the silvery lakes and the mountain ledges.

"Why are we here?" I asked.

"Your she-wolf knows her home. She brought you here. It's a safe spot for her and for you as well." Kadz replied.

"Why were the walls closing in on me at school? I never felt like that before."

"She's ready to come out Lis." Kadz placed his hand on my arm. His touch was soft and comforting.

The bells ringing in my ears rang louder and my vision blurred. Then the breaking began. The pain was unbearable. I was going to die.

Then I heard his voice.

"Just breathe Lis, you can get through this."

Who the hell could get through this pain? I heard myself scream just before I fainted, and the world went black.

When I came to, I saw the tops of the tall trees and the dark blue sky. I rolled over and tried to stand and immediately I fell sideways.

It's okay, Lis. It's difficult to stay on all fours at first.

I heard his laughing voice in my head.

"Four?" I tried to say but instead, a bark came out.

Try to think the words, not speak them out loud. I wondered what your bark would sound like. I like it. It's you, soft and elegant. It fits you perfectly. You're going to be fine, come on, try standing again. Think of it like a crawling human.

I tried to roll over again and tried like an infant to crawl. It worked! I was standing on all four legs. I walked over to the water's edge and looked down. My eyes were yellow, and my fur was the color of burnished copper and long. I turned my head from side to side. My she-wolf looked like me but different. I heard Kadz growl low in his belly and immediately I stepped back towards him. He had his eyes on the trees that lined the far side of the lake. I watched as a smaller wolf emerged and heard a familiar female voice.

You were supposed to watch her, not make her change Kadz. Your alpha told you to be a brother. Lis is off-limits. Who was she that I recognized the sound of her voice? I only knew one other female werewolf, my mom.

Kadz growled.

Transfixed I watched as the little wolf walked confidently towards us around the lake. She shimmered a moment before she stood up on two legs and immediately, I recognized her. Madi.

I passed out once again.

When I came to, Madi and Kadz were on either side of me.

"Madi?" I asked and was grateful I could speak once more.

"Hey Lis, I suppose surprise doesn't cover it this time? Are you okay?" She asked me as she helped me to sit upright.

"Ya, I'm okay." I automatically answered. "Are you a lycanthrope? And why haven't you told me in all the years we have been friends?"

"I wasn't allowed to tell you; I don't belong to Apollo's pack, but I know of him and all of you. I was told to stay apart from others. That I was a lone wolf. My sire left me once I changed. I have been alone for a few years."

"You don't belong on this mountain, leave," Kadz growled.

"You can't tell me where I belong, or who I belong with. You leave. I've been Lis's friend for longer than you have. She probably wouldn't have changed without you bothering her. She could have stayed a human you know." Madi growled back at him.

I was stunned I had never heard her be so aggressive.

"Stop, you two." I interrupted them before it got more heated.

"Kadz, she belongs anywhere she wants to; you won't tell her to leave the mountain or anywhere else. Madi, If you want a pack, you can be in mine." I heard Kadz growl, and I turned to him.

"Madi is my best friend, she's like my sister. If Apollo won't have her then I will leave. Her and I will start our own pack."

"It doesn't work like that Lis." They both said at the same time.

"Well, it should. I guess I need to go speak with Apollo." I told them.

"Maybe you should go home first Lis," Madi said with a smile. "You might need to make yourself a bit more presentable."

I looked down at my tattered blue shirt and my stained capris. Oh no, it was my favorite outfit and I ruined it. My heeled blue sandals were nowhere to be found either.

"Crap. I really liked that shirt." I mumbled.

"You always look nice Lis, and you still smell like coconut to me," Kadz said under his breath as he helped me stand up.

"It's a long way back to my house," I said as I looked up at the darkening sky. "We should get going."

The three of us walked upright, down the mountain. We talked quietly. I asked how many other lone wolves were out there and Madi said there were hundreds. Pack life wasn't for everyone. Which started a conversation about the pros and cons of pack life. I listened as each of them spoke passionately about their lives. There was one heated conversation about mates. Kadz being from the old world said we had mates for life and Madi called him a caveman with old-fashioned values. The lone wolves mated with like-minded lone wolves and separated soon after with no hard feelings. If they stayed together then others would join and that would be pack life. Not lone wolf life. That sounded lonely to me, and I was surprised that Madi was that way. She played soccer and cheered. Both were group activities, not lone-wolf activities. When I asked her about that she said she kept her human life and wolf life totally separate. That her she-wolf had a personality all her own and her human also had other needs, like friends. I thought quietly that that would be difficult to achieve. My wolf was a part of me, I felt whole now that I had let her out, or rather she felt comfortable enough to come out. I couldn't connect with my human life as one anymore, I was a hybrid, I belonged in both worlds while human and wolf.

The walk took longer than I expected, and it was a full moon rise by the time I saw the house lights on.

"I should head home too, Lis," Madi said "You're going to be alright. Kadz thank you for being with her when she changed. It can be scary the first couple of times." She put her hand out to shake his.

"I told Lis, I would be there, whenever she asked," Kadz said as he looked at her and took her small hand in his for a firm shake. "Next time let's plan a run instead of you just showing up ya?" he said.

"Ya." She replied. "See you tomorrow at school Lis."

I watched a moment as she walked into the moonlight and in a split second she was on all fours and running toward town.

"You need to speak to your mom and Apollo, Lis," Kadz said as we approached my old farmhouse. " I need to get some supplies; I will see you tomorrow. Just think of me and I will be there. Good night, Lis, sleep well." He hugged me quickly and sniffed my hair before he turned and disappeared without a sound except for the padded thump of his wolf feet hitting the ground.

"Lis?" I heard my mom as I stepped onto the sagging porch.

"It's me, Mom, sorry I'm late. I left school early and ran to the mountain today."

"I know, the school called to say you were sick and left. Did you go to the mountain alone?"

"Kadz was with me, we ran. I changed mom." I choked out as I sat on the porch swing.

"oh Lis, I'm sorry I wasn't there with you. Are you okay?" she rubbed my arm as I shivered.

"Madi is a lycanthrope."

"What?" she exclaimed.

"Madi is a she-wolf, I saw her. I watched her change. She has been my friend for years and never told me. She was the only person I wanted to tell this morning. She is a lone wolf; she has no pack. She never told me, and I couldn't wait to tell her the truth about me. Why wouldn't she have told me about herself? I guess she wasn't the best friend I always thought her to be. She said her she-wolf has her own personality and prefers to be alone. I fainted when I changed. Kadz was there and got me to stand up without falling over. It was embarrassing. I ruined my good blue shirt and grey capris. I also lost my blue sandals." I cried big wet tears as all the events of the afternoon tumbled out of me.

"It's going to be okay, Lis. I will never leave you. The pack is your family now. Anything you need is yours for the asking. I will talk to Apollo about Madi, maybe he can convince her to stay with the pack. Lis, you will have to make another choice. I'm sorry I didn't tell you before you decided to change." She took a deep breath. "Lis, you are especially important. There has not been a birth in centuries, we have had many changed werewolves but you, you were born a lycanthrope. You were born to be our next leader. The ultima. The leader of every lycanthrope on this earth."

"No. I don't want that. I just want to be human again. I don't want to be a wolf and I want to forget that Madi is a wolf also. Can I go back to that?" I cried.

"Yes. Yes, you can Lis. If it's really what you want." She stroked my hair like she did when I was a child and had hurt myself. "You can make that choice. Remember the pros and cons list we made earlier?" she questioned me.

"Ya. It's changed now though, hasn't it?" I asked.

"Some parts, yes, but for the most part it's the same. Your best friend is a werewolf, you could stay together if she chose to live a pack life. You will need an Alpha and a Beta team of your own. If she is as strong-minded a wolf as you say she is, it might be a good fit for her."

"What if I just want to stay with you and your pack? Do I have to be the big boss? Can't I just be your daughter in the pack too?" I softly questioned her as I thought of different scenarios.

"You don't have to make up your mind today. I asked Apollo to give you till graduation to assimilate into the pack and choose your future path. But you will have to decide, Apollo only gave his permission this one time. His rules are strict, and he never wavers from a choice once it has been made. So, think this through thoroughly. Lis, one more thing to think about. If you choose to be the Ultima, the big boss, I would only be one of your werewolves, you couldn't show any favoritism towards me. It is how the packs work."

"Mom, I don't know what to do. This is for the rest of my life. The rest of our lives. I also think Kadz likes me and wants me as his mate. I'm only seventeen, I don't want a life mate. Madi says he is archaic, and his mated-for-life idea is outdated. Who is right?"

"They both are. I know it's confusing. You have to figure that one out on your own. I think once you decide which life you choose your choices will change with who you mate with. He needs to be someone who will listen to you and also argue with you but only in private. He must stand beside you and rule over the packs and the lone wolves. He must be trustworthy and kind but also strong. It's who I hoped you would choose as a human and also as a wolf." She stood up, "Come on bug, you have had a day, haven't you? Go run a bubble bath, I will bring you up an iced tea. What you need is to have a good night's rest and tomorrow we will go talk with Apollo. He can help you if you have more questions. Come on." She urged me up out of the swing.

"Okay. I guess I am kind of tired, and a bath sounds good." I let her shoulder hug me as we walked to the front door and squeezed through side by side.

Neither of them was aware of the eyes in the dark that followed them, the ears that heard their conversation, or the growl that emitted from the beast within.

CHAPTER NINETEEN

Kadz & Madi

"You waited." He growled as he stopped before her.

"I knew you would come. We've waited long enough. Come on, let's go. We don't need them." Her wolf howled inside to be let out.

"Yes, we do. To have a pack of our own we need her. She's the key." He reached out to her, but she sidestepped him.

"They will smell me on you. You know that." She whispered as she reluctantly stepped back.

"I will have her tomorrow. I will speak with Apollo; she will be my mate and I, her Alpha. He will let us go it only makes sense. He wouldn't be the Alpha if she joined his pack. He will let her go. I know that Gavin has his thoughts on her though, we need to get him out of the picture." Kadz growled the last sentence.

"We weren't supposed to hurt anyone, Kadz. Lis is my friend, and you know I don't have many of those. Promise you will treat her right. She is so fragile. She will need me too." Madi pleaded.

"Tomorrow we will decide everything. Let's go for a run. I miss our time together. I hated watching you with those humans, pretending you were one of them. You are a wolf; you are my wolf." His eyes gleamed bright blue as he looked at her.

She smiled back at him with all the love she had. "Yes, Kadzait, I am yours as you are mine. Forever."

In seconds they were running evenly across the fields, the dry dirt flew as they pounced silently away from the old farmhouse.

CHAPTER TWENTY

Lis

School was dreary the next day, the blistering sun hid behind a thin veil of clouds, giving reprieve from the warmth. Madi called and said she was tired and needed to sleep in so would come to school at lunch. Gabe met me at the bus stop, but I didn't have the energy to talk with him. My mind was going over all sorts of scenarios. I was sure I didn't need a life mate, as Kadz indicated. I knew I had till graduation to make my life choices. At least my mom had said so. She was going to pick me up after school and we were going to speak with Apollo. I hadn't really gotten to know him since I found out about us. I wondered if he would be as intimidating as I had made him out to be.

Twice I had to be asked for my answers from the teacher. I realized I had just sat through my classes. I hadn't listened to a thing. Thankfully, Gabe was there to answer for me. I smiled gratefully at him. He raised his eyebrows in question when the teacher returned to the front of the class. I shrugged my shoulders and gave a small shake of my head.

I called my mom and told her I wanted to meet Apollo at lunch instead of after school. She asked if I was feeling alright. I said I couldn't concentrate on anything, and I might as well deal with what I had to, or I wouldn't be able to think of anything else.

When the bell rang for lunch, I ran to my locker and stuffed my books in it. Gabe was right behind me.

"Hey, Lis. What's going on with you? Are you sick? Madi texted she wasn't feeling well either."

I could hear the concern in his voice. He did care for us. I wonder how he would feel if he found out we had both been lying to him our entire friendship.

"I'm okay, I just have a lot to talk with my mom about. I'm going to meet her right now. I won't be here this afternoon would you mind taking extra good notes for me? I'll stop by your place later on for them." I looked him square in the eye and saw the concern.

"Lis, you've missed more school this month than you have all year. You might not get Valedictorian. Are you sure you should leave today?" I could hear his concern.

"If I don't get it, you will, and I am okay with that Gabe. You deserve it just as much as I do. Probably even more. I'll see you later, okay?" I hugged him and kissed his cheek. "Thank you for caring," I whispered to him as I dashed towards the front doors.

My mom was waiting out front in our old car. I wondered about money and schooling. I needed to figure out my options. I had so many questions and I hoped Apollo could answer all of them. I didn't need more choices, I had to figure out a way to keep everyone happy, including me.

Silently we drove to the hospital. We were told that Dr. Apollo had left early, some sort of family emergency. My mom's lips pressed close together in anger. She rarely got angry and now I understood why, but she was barely holding it together now.

"Mom?" I questioned, "Are you okay? Why are you so angry? It must be something to do with the pack if Apollo said family emergency."

"I should have been called if it has to do with the pack." She ground out between her clenched jaws.

"Oh," I mumbled.

I heard her breathe deeply in and release slowly a few times before I spoke again.

"Are you like the packs' mother? Is Apollo like the dad? To everyone? What do I call him?" I asked quietly, wondering why if he was like their father, why hadn't he been a father figure in my life. I would have liked to have a real father. My mom and I might not have grown so close though. Maybe that was why she kept him away from me.

"Lis," she started. "I am Apollo's Luna, his mate, for life. We are a family. I only kept this part from you so you would know what it would be like to be human. I wanted you to be human for as long as you could be. I wanted you to know that you had a choice in becoming a werewolf. It is still you and me, you will always be my little girl, but I won't be your mom as we know it now. You will change, or you will forget. That can be done. Apollo will explain." She patted my hands as I clenched them together in my lap.

We drove in silence for about an hour. My mind wondering about the amnesia that I could get if I chose to be human. I would keep my friendship with Gabe but what about Madi? Would she leave? She said she was a lone wolf; would that change if I stayed werewolf? How would we be able to keep our friendship?

Slowly we climbed the steep mountain road. Of course, Apollo lived in the mountains. The air was cleaner and crisp. It wasn't the mountain where we ran but another range. We stopped in a large graveled public parking lot about halfway up the mountain. I saw lots of gravel paths along the edges heading up the mountain.

"Okay, here's the thing. To get to Apollo's house you need to be in werewolf form." My mom started.

"Mom!" I cried loudly, "I don't know how to change on purpose. How are we going to get there?"

"I will teach you. It will be okay. You were born for this. You just need to have control."

"Are we going to sit here in the open? In the car? Where are we going?" I nervously asked.

"Come on." She said as she unclipped her seat belt. "I would like to see my beautiful daughter embrace her wolf."

I could hear her excitement as she spoke.

We locked the car up and left our running shoes inside.

"First things first Lis. You can preserve your clothing. They might get rumpled or dirty, but you can keep from tearing them. I usually keep a brush in my bag as well as emergency things. Tweezers are helpful when you start, there are a lot of thorns and branches around the ground. Having fruit or veggies before you change keeps the hunger at bay for longer than a bag of chips or popcorn would." She handed me an apple and a granola bar. "You can listen to the world around you before you change, listen to the animals, they will let you know if any humans are around. You can taste the air, the temperature, the humidity, or lack of it, it will let you know how safe you are when you change. Thunderstorms are awful to run in, you can barely hear the rest of the pack with all the rain, wind, and thunder. The full moon is obviously the easiest time to change and run. The humans are more lenient of us then, it's like they know deep down that the werewolves love the moon, and they don't report us to the authorities." She paused took a deep breath and looked at me.

"You are special in so many ways, Lis." Her hand reached up and smoothed back my hair. "I have not lived while there was an Ultima wolf, your abilities will be much the same but also so much more. You will be faster, and stronger and you will also have the ability to change a human to a werewolf. We can change humans as well, but we have to scratch them and they have to have our blood in them when they change to become full werewolves, I believe you will be able to change them just by thinking about it. It is a big responsibility, but I know you can handle it. Now, let's go sit over there." She gestured to a small trail I had barely seen.

We walked over and I thought about how many people I could change if I only had to think about it. I would need to make sure that I knew how to keep that under control. I giggled and my mom looked at me with inquiring eyes.

"Sorry Mom, I was just thinking how many wolves there would be if I only had to think about changing them. We would really have a large family then hu?" I laughed at her expression. "I'm only kidding Mom. Relax, I will be fine."

She smiled but said nothing. Once we were settled and had eaten our little snacks, we laid down on our backs and looked at the sky. The clouds had receded, and the sun once again blazed down on the dry cracked land. We had so much rain the last year and now it just stopped. It didn't take long for the thirsty ground to soak up the liquid. I wondered if we would get rain again.

Calmly we lay side by side in silence. Our breathing matched as we watched the clouds drift around the sky. We listened to the birds sing to each other and the squirrels chittered as they scrambled from tree to tree.

Lis? Can you hear me?

"Yes," I answered my mom out loud.

Don't say it out loud, just think of me and whisper it. She replied.

I thought of my beautiful mom, how caring she was, how it had been just the two of us for so long. I felt my eyes burn with tears and quickly blinked them away. I thought of her smile and the way she smelled her coffee before she took her first hot sip.

YES, I HEAR YOU MOM! It was so loud she jumped beside me and held my hand.

It's okay, you are just trying really hard. Just relax and try to think about how we speak to each other daily. There's no need to yell. The closer we are in connection the easier it will be to talk like this. You might need a bit of practice with the other members of the pack as you don't know them. Yet.

Okay, I can do this. I heard Gavin and Kadz like this. Oh, I also heard Apollo one time. It's like there are people in my brain. Can they read my mind? I questioned.

No, your thoughts are still your private thoughts, until you think about sharing them and you will need to think about the person for them to hear you. It's like visually sharing your thoughts. It takes a bit of practice, but I know you will be able to do it. Now about your clothing. When you change, just before you feel the first bone stretch, you need to think about a bag or a purse or some type of pack something that can hold your clothing inside it. It isn't a physical object but one you can visualize. Can you see one? She asked.

Yup, I got one. It's the red backpack in the back of my closet. It…

Lis? My mom interrupted, *You don't need to tell me which bag it is, you just need to visualize it for yourself. Now that you have a picture of it think of your clothing folded up inside the bag. You got it? Okay now here is the tricky part. You need to get the clothing inside the bag just before you change, or you will be naked. Do you have all this visualized?*

I got it Mom, bag, clothing inside, keep that picture right up until the first bone stretches.

Right, okay now smell the air. Do you smell the iron tang of any humans? The smell of dogs around you? Listen, do you hear any vehicles, planes, trains?

She waited a minute so I could get my bearings and smell the air. It smelled like trees. I listened closely and heard nothing but the pattering of tiny feet. Little forest animals but no human sounds.

Okay, are you ready Lis? she asked.

Ready, I answered. I thought of the bag, and I thought about changing into my wolf. I felt the stretch of my legs and closed my eyes. I could do this.

Open your eyes, Lis. She instructed.

I opened one eye and looked at the sky. Then I saw her in my peripheral, she was beautiful. Her hair was brushed and shiny. Her eyes were yellow like mine were but mine were bright like neon whereas hers were like buttercup yellow. Her dark lashes framed the oval shape. She was just as beautiful in wolf form as she was in human form.

Stand up, Lis. She whispered. *Stand tall and let me see you.*

I remembered Kadz telling me to think like I was walking on all fours. I stumbled a bit but got up. I was bigger than my mom. Much bigger. I shook my head and smiled. I felt free. I wanted to run. I turned towards the hidden path and took a step but stopped to look back at my mom. She was stone still, watching me.

I want to run. I told her. My voice was different. I would think about that later. *Let's go.* I thought to her, and she nodded her head quickly in agreement.

Together we took off, I heard the pounding of my paws on the uneven path. It wasn't long before I was much further ahead of my mom. I didn't want to slow down. I didn't want to wait. I was free. I was finally free to run. I smelled the air as it whipped past my snout. Sweet. The air smelled sweet.

Lis? I heard my mom. *You're too fast for me. Apollo is waiting at the chalet on the East side of the mountain. He's excited to meet you.*

I barely heard her over the wolf that howled inside of me. In moments I smelled another werewolf. Was it Apollo? I stretched my legs and kept running. Apollo would have to wait if he wanted to meet me. I wasn't ready to stop yet. I sensed another wolf, and heard the pounding of the paws, matching mine. I could feel the heat of the breath as the wolf pulled up beside me, in silence we ran. I could feel the heat from the large black wolf, the sweat as we climbed. Something else as well, anticipation? I wasn't sure but it felt good. I stumbled and the black wolf pounced, we rolled thunderously through the trees, knocking down everything in our path. When we stopped, I was lying flat on my back, human and naked. Where were my clothes? I felt the body on top of me tense. I pushed him off and watched as Gavin smiled down at me and reached his hand out to help me up. He was gorgeous. His mop of black hair covered one eye and he shook his head back to uncover his green eyes and half of his face.

"Hi, Lis. Nice to see you again." He growled.

"Gavin. Hey. Little help with my clothes. Please." I begged him.

"Sure. Whatever you need gorgeous." He easily replied. Like he was used to naked females just standing around talking to him.

"It's just skin, Lis. You need to get used to being in it if you're going to be changing into your she-wolf constantly."

"I would love to have a conversation with you Gavin, but first, my clothes."

"Would you be more at ease if I just took mine off too?" he asked innocently.

I looked at his black t-shirt and hip-hugging jeans. The guy was just too incredible to be human. I quickly remembered that he wasn't human. He was a lycanthrope just like me.

"Just help me with my clothes, Gavin" I sighed exasperated.

"Close your eyes and think of where you packed your clothes away. Think about taking them and putting them on piece by piece." His voice growled low, and my belly shook with something.

What was that emotion? Like longing or belonging. I closed my eyes and I saw our bodies as we collided as wolves, how safe I felt even as we crashed through the trees. He had wrapped himself around me to keep me from getting hurt. I felt his hand as he lifted my hair off my neck and put it gently outside the collar of my shirt. I stepped towards him, and he held me tight for a moment. His breath at my ear. I heard him growl low before he nuzzled his face to my neck, and I held my breath. Then he licked my heated neck. I felt shivers all the way down to my human toes. My she-wolf pushed to get out. I had to stop her. Slowly I took a step back. Gavin watched me with golden eyes. His wolf was close to the surface as well.

"Apollo is waiting for me. We should go." I said softly as I retreated another step.

"Apollo can wait all night. Lis, we need to talk. I know you feel something for me. I feel it too, you are not just like my sister. You are meant for me, our wolves know it, they feel it."

"No, I don't even know who my she-wolf is. I need time to get to know how to navigate this new life. I'm only seventeen. My birthday isn't for a few more days. I am not ready to make a life mate choice. I have so many choices to make. Please don't make me choose you yet. Just be my friend."

"Kadz" I heard him mumble under his breath as he inhaled and let out a long slow breath. "friends? I'm not sure my wolf can do that, but I can. For now." He said a bit louder.

"Do you know where we are?" I asked him as I looked around the forest.

"A couple of mountain ranges to the West of Apollo's mountain. Do you want to walk, get a piggyback, or change?" He questioned me.

"I'm not sure if I can control my wolf around you. I am also a bit tired from the change and the long run. Piggyback?" I asked with a grin.

"I like your wolf as well, but I can piggyback you if that's what you want." He grinned back.

I liked this fun side of him.

"Jump on, your ride awaits." He turned his back to me, and I jumped up and wrapped my legs around his waist and my arms circled his neck. He smelled nice. I lay my head on his back and hung on as he started walking.

We talked for hours, the darkening sky led us back across the fields, streams, and rocks until we arrived back on Apollos' mountain. Gavin wasn't even winded. I had walked for brief periods, but he had mostly carried me. I felt like I knew him, and I felt very safe when I was with him. He told me about the pack, how he and my mom were Apollo's betas, and what that meant. Why they had to be doctors when they were human. The lycanthropes didn't work at normal jobs. They had to do small jobs some even worked for a job temp service, only taking jobs when they needed to. Apollo, Gavin, and my mom worked at the hospital in senior positions so they could come and go as they pleased. They also made money for the pack. They shared all their material goods in their human form. The pack life was different. There was a hierarchy with Apollo at the top, Gavin and my mom equally below him. However, when Apollo was gone, my mom was the pack leader with Gavin her second. That was because my mom was the Luna to Apollo. I wondered where I would fit in. I wondered if Apollo would accept my wolf. I hadn't met the whole pack but if they were all as intimidating as Gavin and Kadz were I wondered where I would fit in with them too. I thought about Madi. I was still hurt she hadn't told me about herself. When I asked Gavin if he knew about her, he hesitated before he answered.

"We always know when lone wolves are around, they don't want a pack life for whatever reason. She kept to herself and didn't reveal her true self to you, so we didn't intervene with your friendship. We would have, had she tried to tell you anything. Your mom was adamant, her one unbreakable rule was that we leave you alone until you were ready to learn about us, about your true self."

"I met you before I knew who you were, and before I knew who and what I was. You came into my house like you owned it. Do you?" I questioned him.

"The house is ours, yes. The whole pack. We call it our communal house. The house is far enough away from everyone that our howls don't cause concern. The field is easy to run in and it is close to the mountain ledges where we meet. The lake is our pool, and the mountain is our playground. The humans don't know about us here. If they do, they don't let it bother them. We don't interfere in their lives, and they don't in ours. Of course, they are not entirely sure that we exist, the lycanthropes. They know there are wolves in the mountains they just don't know we are also a part of their town. Their doctors, nurses, paramedics." He paused his words a moment.

I watched him as he looked up the mountain. My eyes traveled as far as his to see a lone figure standing on the precipice watching us. Apollo.

Gavin had told me about his real family, how he was the afterthought to all of them. The youngest. He told me he was from a family of Gods who had fantastic abilities, they all did, except for him. He was tired of being left out.

Gently he let me down and I clung to his back. Once my feet landed softly on the dirt, I let go of him only to find his hand and grip it tightly. I needed him beside me as I went to meet my Alpha. I felt his rough hand gently squeeze mine and he tugged me along as we stepped towards the silent figure waiting for us.

CHAPTER TWENTY-ONE

Apollo

It was happening. All the choices we had given her, she had chosen Gavin. I knew they belonged together and watching them walk together I knew it was right. He treated her like his partner even though she was human, and he was a God. She had no idea how much her world was going to change. She had accepted this life with ease. Rhea had taught her to be kind and thoughtful. She would be a great leader. With Gavin beside her, they would lead the lycanthrope world together. In this world and the others as well. Gavin needed a title of his own, he was ready to lead. Lis would be his partner.

Apollo? Have they arrived yet? I heard Rhea ask quietly.

I looked back at her. She was my love. I had to tell her about me before I could tell Lis about her new path with Gavin. I had never told Rhea that I was a God. She loved me, obeyed me, fought with me, enchanted me. Would she love me when she knew I was not from this world?

Come, Rhea, let's walk a bit. Gavin and Lis will be here shortly, and I need a moment with just you. I held out my hand and she took it. I watched as she shivered, my touch electric to her human body. We walked to the far side of the lawn atop the mountain. The chalet lit the evening with the lights glowing from within. This was a perfect spot. Some days I knew why my brother Tyler, chose to stay at the top of his mountain. I hoped he was happy with his new bride, Ava, and her brother, Freedom, who had chosen to stay and learn about his gypsy magic. They would have to meet Rhea and Lis.

Apollo? She questioned me.

"Rhea, love, I haven't been honest with you about all things. Let me be quick and tell you, that I love you. I will always love you even if you choose to leave me."

"Why would I leave you? Apollo, what's going on?" she looked at me with alarmed eyes.

I had to just tell her and if she believed me, it would be all right, there just wasn't going to be an easier way.

"I'm not from this world Rhea." I gazed into her eyes, willing her to trust me, to trust my wolf.

"What do you mean?" she looked trustingly into my wolf eyes.

"I have siblings who have realms. My brother Ian is a Gatekeeper.

Meaning he guards the gates that open to other worlds. He lets those who need to travel, through each door to wherever they are going. My other brother, Tyler, just married a witch. He is the God of magic in all our worlds. I am also a God. I am the god of the supernatural, the werewolves, vampires, Loch Ness, and leprechauns, among others. I and my siblings made this world and all the living things in it." I stopped as I heard the intake of her breath, she slipped her hand from mine and turned her back to me. I was her Alpha; she had never done that before. I wouldn't have let her. This news, however, would be a shock to anyone so I let her think a moment and I let her turn her back to me. Silently I held my breath.

"Gods? Lis? Myself? Why us? What are you doing with us? What about Gavin, you said he was your brother. Is he a God of something?" She whispered without looking at me.

I knew she was thinking about Lis out there with Gavin, all alone.

"Gavin is a God as well. There is going to be a change, Rhea. He will be given his own realm. He wasn't ready before, but he is now. Lis has changed something in him. She has made him softer, and more appreciative of the world he lives in. He cares for her and would treat her like his queen if she chooses him. I believe she has Rhea. I watched them together today. They belong together, as humans and as lycanthropes."

"But you're not human, are you?" Rhea interrupted as she finally turned back to me. I noticed she didn't meet my eyes. "you or Gavin? Your Gods, not humans, not even Lycanthropes."

"Rhea, didn't you hear what I said? My brother loves a human, a witch. Ian also has a human girlfriend. Enid is her name. Well, she isn't all the way human, but she is close and has been raised here in this world. The point is that they know about us, and they choose to be together. They understand that we wouldn't hurt anyone. We love this world, we love the people, the animals, the flora, the fauna. We aren't here to harm anyone. The opposite actually. We make sure the humans have all the choices they need. We make sure that good and evil are equal so the inhabitants can coexist. Rhea, we have always been here. Please look at me. Let me see your eyes."

Slowly I waited for her to turn her eyes my way. My heart ached when I saw the unshed tears hovering in her eyes. Her wolf was gone. Her eyes were brown.

"Rhea, nothing has to change between us. You are still my Luna, my mate, my partner. I need you. I love you as I have loved you for years."

"Everything has changed, Apollo. Everything."

I watched her walk away from me. Meeting Gavin and Lis at the chalet I saw her put her hand out and Lis took it. They walked away, together. Gavin looked at me and turned to follow them.

"Stop Gavin, let them go. Let them go." I ordered.

"Apollo, brother, what have you done?" Gavin questioned me with accusing eyes.

"I told Rhea the truth. I told her the truth about us, and she walked away. She walked away from me." I had never felt so empty in all my life.

CHAPTER TWENTY-TWO

Rhea

A God. I had been living a life with a God for fifteen years and he never thought he could trust me with this information. Would he have even told me if I hadn't had Lis? Was he only with me because of Lis, he knew she was special. Had he made her? Designed her? Was she even a part of me anymore? I looked at her and saw the worry in her eyes. Yes, she was still a part of me. The best part I hoped. Gavin was also a God. Did Lis know that? Was it my responsibility to tell her?

"Lis, Apollo, and I had a little disagreement. Sorry that you still haven't gotten to know him. I know we were supposed to have a BBQ. I'm not sure when that will happen. He wants to know you, as a wolf. He will come around in a day or two, okay? You spent a lot of time with Gavin today. Did you learn anything new? How far did you run? You sure are fast and your legs are much longer than mine. You are a beautiful wolf, Lis. I knew you would be."

We sat side by side on the porch swing. Slowly rocking. The night had been long. It was nearing midnight.

"I learned a lot about pack life. That you are the boss when Apollo is away. Where will I fit into the pack? I like Gavin. I don't have to think about who I want to be with mom. It has been Gavin since I met him. I just had my head turned by Kadz, but he isn't my mate for life. Gavin is my choice. He is kind and listens to me and he answered all the questions I had. He made me feel safe, we laughed easily, and we argued a little bit as well, but it was okay. We each understand that everyone needs different things to be happy."

"Did he tell you that he was different? Him and Apollo and their siblings?" I asked her quietly.

"Different?" Lis asked, "Mom, they are Gods, like real Greek Gods. They designed the earth and other worlds as well. It's so cool. I can't wait to visit some of the other places. Not just outside of North America but outside this realm. I can't wait to meet Ava and Enid. They sound kick ass! They stopped the world from flooding and broke a chant that had been around for hundreds of years. Can you believe that we can travel to different worlds? We just have to walk through a doorway that Ian opens for us. Gavin didn't think you knew any of this."

I watched the light in Lis's eyes twinkle, they were golden, and her wolf was happy. I wondered if I would see my blue-eyed girl again. She had grown up so much in the last week. It wasn't just her and I any longer. She had chosen a mate. A God. Where did that leave me?

CHAPTER TWENTY-THREE
Kadz

Something had changed. I thought of the she-wolf asleep on my bed, her hair spread out on the pillows. Madi claimed to be a lone wolf, but she needed me. I settled down and closed my eyes bringing her closer to me she wiggled and nestled into my arms content to sleep till the morning.

I heard a snap, I was dreaming. I was on the mountain. A pack meeting? Now? In the middle of the night. I should still be in bed with the little she-wolf wrapped around me.

I glanced around as the members of the pack entered the dream meeting. We sat on our ledges patiently waiting for Apollo to start. I noticed Rhea was absent.

Gavin stood arrogantly beside Apollo. He met my gaze and growled. I bowed my head in deference to his position. How I hated that part of pack life. As a human, I could whip his ass but as a werewolf, I had to follow protocol. I twitched as I saw the grin on his snout.

Good evening to you all, thank you for coming so late. I know you would all rather be asleep right now.

Something was off, Apollo's wolf timber sounded hollow. What was going on? I perked my ears up to listen. Lifting my snout, I smelled her. Lis was here. Once more I met Gavin's stare. In seconds I knew why he had smiled. She stood beside him. Beautiful. Elegant. Perfect. No! She had chosen him. He smirked because he had won her. She was supposed to choose me. I was the perfect match for her. There was only one way to make that happen. I tensed my muscles to pounce but stopped as Apollo started to speak once more.

I have to leave on extended business, Rhea is busy as well, so I leave Gavin in charge. As well, we have a new member of the pack, Lis, please come forward and meet everyone.

She stepped softly forward and bowed low to him before she turned to us all.

Hi everyone, thank you for accepting me into your pack. I look forward to talking with you all one-on-one, as a human and a werewolf. This life is new to me so I may have a lot of questions.

She took a step back to be behind Gavin and Apollo respectively bowing her head as she moved.

Her red coat gleamed in the moonlight and as she looked to Apollo her yellow eyes sparkled. It wasn't fair. She should be mine. She was perfect. I had waited for her to choose me; I should have just taken her when I had the chance.

I looked at Gavin and he silently watched me with those haughty eyes. How I hated him. I growled low and dangerously. I gave him fair warning before I pounced towards his smirking face. I would rip him limb from limb for taking my chance at being her mate. The large black werewolf snarled as he met me and together, we ripped at each others' throats. We flew through the air tearing at each other trying to find a vulnerable spot. Our snouts snapped loudly as they tore into each other's flesh. I felt blood flow out of my shoulder as Gavin took a chunk. I howled loudly and shook my head. I rammed his side, and we tumbled over the ledge landing loudly on a rocky precipice. Breathing hard, we circled one another each of us searching for a vulnerable spot. My hind leg slipped on the shale rock, and I listened as pieces tumbled down the rocky slope.

NO, we heard a thundering voice call out above us.

I wobbled as I tried to stand. My head wouldn't lift off the ground. What was this? I looked at Gavin and his head was bowed low to the ground as well. But he looked peaceful, not agitated.

No Kadz, no Gavin. There will be no more fighting on this night. Not over me.

I looked up at her, she stood so regal. Her ruffle stood up around her shoulders and her eyes were the blood red of the Ultima. I knew Lis was special. I didn't know she would turn out to be the Ultima.

Kadzait, I have chosen Gavin to be my mate. My partner in human and werewolf forms. No more challenges will be issued.

She was magnificent. I would do whatever she asked of me. I tore my gaze from her quickly and looked around at the pack. They all had their heads bowed low for her. Even Gavin stood lower than he had just minutes before. Apollo stood apart, already he had left our pack. The control was in Lis's hands. No one, not even an Alpha would disobey the Ultima.

Silently I nodded my head in deference to her. I would have to leave the pack. I couldn't obey Gavin; I couldn't obey her.

Slowly the pack lifted their heads. Lis sat on the ground watching us as Gavin went through the rest of the pack meeting. No one questioned where Rhea was.

When it was time to go the sun was just lightening the sky. Lis came to me, and I looked at her. No longer were her eyes the red of the Ultima, she had the yellow eyes I had seen on her first change. The girl I loved was in there still.

Kadz, are you okay? Will you be okay with me? With us? I love you as a brother, as a friend. You belong with our pack family.

Lis, I knew you were special, I didn't know you were going to be the Ultima. I will take the memory of your first change with me always. If you need me just call out, I will come but I cannot stay and be happy for you with Gavin. He doesn't know you, Lis. Not like I do. He wasn't there for you when you changed the first time. I was. I know in my heart we are meant to be together, but I will not stand in your way with Gavin. All I want is for you to be happy.

Be safe Kadz, I hope you find your life mate. I'm sorry if I hurt you.

I stepped back a moment to look at her once more before I closed my eyes and returned to the sleeping, she-wolf in my bed.

I opened my eyes when she started moving about. I guess it was time to get up.

"Kadz, why are you all bloody?" Madi asked me when she sat up.

"Had a little run-in with Gavin. It's okay now. We should pack up and get moving. We don't need this pack any longer."

"What about Lis?" Madi questioned as I walked into the bathroom to shower.

"Can't have her. She chose Gavin. Did you know she was the Ultima wolf?" I stepped under the hot water and watched as blood swirled around the drain.

"WHAT!" Madi screamed as she ripped open the shower curtain.

"Madi, close the curtain," I said slowly before she could ask again.

"So let me get this straight," Madi excitedly continued as she slowly closed the shower curtain, "Gavin and Lis are an item, for life. Lis is also the Ultima. More powerful than any Alpha out there. I wonder if she will finish school. I better get moving if I want to meet her at the bus stop. See you later Kadz."

She bounced out of the bathroom, and I heard her get ready to get to school. How human of her.

CHAPTER TWENTY-FOUR

Lis & Madi

I was so tired but energized at the same time. I hadn't slept a wink last night after the meeting. I had stayed and talked with Apollo and Gavin. I knew my mom was upset with them for not telling her that they were Gods. I still got the shivers as I thought about that. I might have chosen to be the Ultima wolf tonight, but I knew that the Gods were senior to me. We couldn't let the pack know about them though, so Gavin had conceded to be my Beta, at least in front of the pack. I had a lot to learn but Apollo had assured me that I would lead the packs around the world with ease.

I smiled as I saw Madi practically bouncing beside Gabe as they waited for my bus to stop.

"Hey, you guys." I greeted them as I stepped onto the sidewalk.

"Well, you both look a lot better than you did yesterday. I hope I don't get sick. We have a major test coming up today, Lis, you missed out on the notes and practice test we did yesterday in class. Just sit by me and I will help you if you need it." Gabe said although he did have dark circles under his eyes. I hope he was feeling good enough to stay the day at school.

"Thanks, Gabe, you're the best. I should be okay though." I touched his arm feeling his heat through his light jacket. "You're sure your okay Gabe? " I questioned. "You feel a bit warm," I said as I started walking to the doors.

I stopped suddenly as I heard a howl, like a child. I looked at Madi and she smiled at me, oblivious to the pain I had heard. I shook my head. If Madi couldn't hear it, then I must be dreaming.

"I'm good. Come on we don't want to be late." Gabe smiled as he grabbed my hand and pulled me along behind him.

The day was like any other, we shared our lunches, and we went to classes. We wanted to go for a sundae after school, but Gabe said his stomach ached and he headed home.

We both told him to not get sick. Then left the school as he boarded his school bus.

That gave Madi and me some time to catch up. We walked slowly to the restaurant making sure Bessie wasn't around to hear us talk. The gossip she would spread if she heard us would be unbelievable. The vinyl benches crinkled as we sat in a booth far from the other customers.

We talked about everything. Except that Gavin and Apollo were Gods. That wasn't a part of my story to tell. I asked Madi to stay with my pack, I needed a Zeta. An independent and sharp wolf who could lead the pack in times of stress. She said she had to think about it and talk with Kadz. I was surprised to hear that she knew him. She told me that he had wanted me to be his mate so he could have the power of an Alpha. They hadn't known I was going to be the Ultima. She tried to call him and let him know where she was, but he hadn't answered. She didn't have the mind speak that we did, she wasn't a part of our pack.

I tried to reach out to him, but I also didn't get an answer.

I made sure to tell Madi that I was so glad she was my friend and that she was there for me to talk with. We giggled like the teenage girls we were. I had missed her. Our friendship had changed but she was still the cheerleader, and her bubbly personality soon had me laughing.

All too soon, we had to leave. We still had parents and they made the rules for the human girls we were. Madi's parents arrived first, and we hugged goodbye.

As I waited for my mom to pick me up, I heard the howl of a child. I looked around and once again noticed no one else had heard it. What was going on?

I heard the rumbling of our old car as it came down the street. We needed a new one, I would ask Apollo about that when I saw him next.

"Hi, Mom." I greeted her as I opened the rusted door. "Are there such things as werewolf cubs? I swear I hear a baby cry every once in a while."

"Hi bug," she replied "No, there aren't any lycanthrope babies. You were the first one born into the pack for centuries. Why? Is there something you want to tell me?" She questioned with her eyebrows raised high into her hairline.

"No, Mom. I am not having a baby. I swear I just heard one crying. Madi didn't hear it although I didn't get a chance to ask her. Is it normal to hear stuff like that?" I wondered.

"Lis, I'm afraid anything you experience might not be normal for anyone else. You're special. If you want, we could ask Apollo. I haven't seen him today but I'm sure he would answer any questions you have."

"Mom, I'm not one to give anyone dating advice, seeing as I have only had one boyfriend, but Apollo trusted you enough to tell you everything about him and you turned your back on him. He might not be a human, but he still has human feelings. He loves you and he needs you. I think you should have a talk with him and clear up any questions you might have. Gavin and I have talked for hours. He's told me all about his family, he's like the black sheep, but I have a feeling once he takes control of the lycanthrope families with me, he will get a bit more appreciation from his brothers and sisters. You should go to the chalet and make Apollo dinner and have a talk."

"Lis, honey. Take the car home. I need to be someplace." She instructed me as we pulled over to the side of the road.

I removed my seatbelt and leaned over to kiss my mom on the cheek.

"You're growing up my girl. You're right. I need to speak with Apollo. See you tonight. I won't need dinner." My mom explained as she rushed out of the stopped car

My little girl was growing up. She was right. I had left my mate to be alone. He had trusted me, he had trusted me to raise Lis on our own, he trusted me to look after our pack when he was gone away, he trusted me with his truth, and I had abandoned him. I needed to talk with him.

"See you, Mom. Good Luck. Love you." I called to her as I watched her take off running across the field towards the mountain and to the man she loved.

I got out of the car and sat in the driver's seat. It was hot and our air conditioner in the car quit working a couple of summers ago. I unrolled the driver's window and fastened my seatbelt. I heard it again. The crying baby. It was frustrating. There should be no crying babies out here. Was I going crazy?

CHAPTER TWENTY-FIVE
Gavin & Lis

I drove home and wasn't surprised to see Gavin sitting on the front porch waiting for me.

"Hello beautiful, how was your day?" He greeted me as he opened the car door.

"Hey, is it normal to hear crying babies? I swear the sound has followed me around all day." I answered him.

"I hear lots of different sounds, it might not be a baby, but there haven't been any were-babies born so it can't be that. Of course, your hearing must be magnified not only as a wolf but as the Ultima as well. You might just be hearing babies from the hospital or something."

"I don't think what I'm hearing is human babies, Gavin. I feel like there's a difference in those cries. It's almost haunting. It gives me the shivers." I gave a little shake as I said it.

"Come on you must need a run after being cooped up all day in that cement building of a school. Isn't it your birthday?" he casually asked.

"What? Today? Well, I guess it is, my mom and I don't celebrate our birthdays. We usually have a big dinner but no presents, no balloons, no cake. We like it better like that; however, I did tell my mom to go see Apollo and to make him dinner and have a talk. So, no celebration dinner tonight. It's just you and me. Do you eat? Or does it taste like dust as you said your brothers don't eat much. I've seen you eat." I looked at him as we climbed the rickety stairs.

"I eat, it's different for me than my siblings. I came after them, I guess you could say I am a perfected version of them all. They all have faults, things that could hurt them, a disability of some sort. I don't have that, as far as I know. My parents had time to correct any faults by the time I came around. I am the most perfect being you will meet." He wriggled his eyebrows as I looked at him.

"You are not perfect, no one is." I reminded him as we walked into the house. "Gavin, is it just me or is it cooler these days? I don't seem to be as wilted or hot and sweaty as I was. The temperature is just as hot as it was last week. Is it a wolf thing?"

"Yes, it's a wolf thing." He answered smiling at me. "You won't get hot or cold. The temperature you are right now is how you will be for all time. Even if you were in the Amazon jungle or the Arctic Circle. Clothing is always optional when you're a wolf. The European wolves hang out around the clothing-optional pools. There are whole colonies that never wear clothes. Freedom at its' finest right there. Want to try it?" He questioned innocently.

"No." I answered, "I am just getting used to changing…just being a lycanthrope in general. I do not want or need more challenges right now. Now I also learned that I am the Ultima. Gavin, I am the leader of the lycanthropes all over the world. That's huge. I don't know if I can do it. What happens if there is fighting or anything like that? I know Apollo explained what he could last night, but I'm still nervous." I looked into his eyes and begged silently for reassurance.

"Lis, you were born for this. Your legacy has been waiting for you for years. Your mom and Apollo have trained you to lead whether you knew it or not. With me by your side to help in any way. We can do this. You can do this. I will always have your back, no matter what. Okay?"

"Okay," I replied. His reassurance was just what I needed. "Let's have a quick bit to eat, go for a run, and then I have homework to finish." I watched as he rolled his eyes.

"You don't need to do homework, Lis."

"Yes, I do. I am almost finished school and I need to finish that." I replied as I grabbed peanut butter and jam to make some sandwiches.

As birthday suppers went it was pretty small. A couple of sandwiches and some iced tea. What came after was the best present. A run with my boyfriend. We ran the mountainside, swam in the lake, and lazed around in a flower-filled field talking about the future. I spoke of school. My Valedictorian speech, which I hadn't finished, and the lycanthrope world. The vision we had to shape our community. How we could help any newcomers fit into the human and werewolf world. The balance it needed. Maybe we could bring to light the wolf community and see how the humans felt about us. We have lived in our community for a long time and almost everyone knew of us as humans we thought about how they would accept us as werewolves. Maybe there were others that we didn't know about, like Madi, she was a lone wolf, and no one knew she was a wolf until I had changed. She had known me forever and had kept the secret. I told Gavin that I had asked Madi to be my Zeta, she would still be a bit of a loner, but she would always have backup if she joined the pack. He liked the idea. Gavin agreed that it was best to have a solid group of leaders and he had seen Madi take charge in the human world and said she would be a natural Zeta for us.

When the stars started poking out, I said we had to head back, I still had a bit of homework to finish. He helped me stand up and held me close a minute longer before his head bent towards mine.

He kissed me until I saw stars in my head. Panting we broke apart and I placed my palm on his heaving chest and pushed him a step back, "Gavin, I need to know who I am first before anything more can happen between us. I need you as a brother, friend, a life-long mate. I am sorry I can't give you everything right now. Please be patient with me." I looked into his eyes.

"Lis, I will wait forever for you. You are my life-long mate, I know it, and I will wait for you to know it too."

He hugged me close to him and I listened as our heartbeats slowed to normal and he kissed my hair.

"Come on, I can help you with your homework if you need it." He smirked as he said it. He knew it was easy for me. "I can make you some popcorn while you finish your homework." He tugged my hand, and we started running back down the mountain. The run cooled us off and we howled as we tumbled down the mountain across the field and saw the dark farmhouse silhouette growing bigger as we neared it.

We noticed the dark mound lying across the steps at the same time. It wasn't moving. Was that a body? We smelled the metallic tang of blood at the same time and bounded forward.

CHAPTER TWENTY-SIX

Lis

"Oh no, Madi!" I noticed her hair first. It was matted with dark red blood. I ran to her and touched her arm. I heard her moan. "What happened? Madi are you okay? Madi, can you hear me?" I hurled questions at her shaking body. Gently I tried to turn her over, but I couldn't move her. She was dead weight.

"Gavin?" I questioned as I looked around me.

"I'm here," he answered from the doorway. He had grabbed the blanket from the couch. "Let me get her inside." He bent down to wrap her in the blanket before gently lifting her and carrying her still body inside.

"Mom?" I called out but didn't get an answer. She must still be with Apollo at the cabin. The house lights were all off, so I turned the living room lamp on, and soft light illuminated the walls.

I watched as Gavin placed Madi on the old couch. I heard her moan again. I went to the kitchen and wet a towel.

"Madi? What happened? Please wake up." I begged her as I wiped her face with the towel. The blood was smeared with dirt. Where had this happened? Why had it happened? I remembered that just a few hours ago we had been laughing and being teenagers and now she was beaten down and bloodied. While Gavin and I had been running around and talking she had been beaten. I should have been there to help her.

I noticed Gavin sitting in the armchair beside the couch. He was stone cold, eyes closed. Like a statue.

"Lis?" Madi mumbled. "Lis, he's going to kill you."

"Who? Who did this Madi and who is going to kill me?" I asked but Madi had already passed out again.

I waited patiently for Gavin to come back to me. He told me he was able to communicate with his family through telepathy. He would be talking with Apollo. I hoped he would have some answers. I took inventory of what I could see, hear, and smell. The distinctive coppery smell of Madi's blood overwhelmed almost everything else. There were no sounds other than our beating hearts, and the creaking old farmhouse. No one was here, no one was nearby. It was just the three of us. I started shaking and drew in some deep breaths. Madi needed me. I couldn't fall apart.

"Lis, Apollo has no idea what happened. Madi will have to wake up and tell us what she can. Your mom and Apollo are on their way here now." Gavin knelt on the wooden floor and eased the bloody towel from my hands. He stood up and kissed my head as he passed by.

In minutes he was back with a fresh towel and a bowl of warm water. I watched as he gently washed Madi's dirty hands and cleaned the deep scratches. Tenderly he went to her feet and washed them as well. We waited patiently for Madi to come around. We needed to hear what had happened to her. Who it was that told her I would be next? Why would someone want to kill me? I just met all the pack members, no one in town had any reason to hurt me or Madi. It didn't make any sense. Gavin and I quietly discussed the who's and why's. In minutes we looked up in surprise as Apollo and my mom walked in. We hadn't heard them at all. Not even their heartbeats. It should have taken them longer to get here from the mountain.

I looked closer at my mom. She had a sickly green pallor instead of her usually glowing skin.

"Mom, are you okay? Are you sick?" I stood up as she entered the living room.

"I'm okay bug. Are you okay? How is Madi doing? Has she woken up again?" My mom answered as she lowered herself to the end of the couch by Madi's feet.

Gavin and Apollo went back outside, and I heard them as they walked around our farmhouse. I heard the deep mumbles of their voices as they discussed the events of the past weeks.

"Mom," I whispered. "How did you get home so fast from the mountain?"

"Apollo opened a doorway, we stepped through, and suddenly I was at the front doorway to the house. I have never been so scared. I just thought of you and how scared you must have been to see Madi lying on our steps, and I knew I had to get home. Apollo said no human had ever gone through a doorway like that. He didn't know how I was able to do it. It must be what he and Gavin are talking about right now."

The color was returning to her cheeks, and I felt better about that. She got up and hugged me tightly and said how glad she was that I was okay. Thank goodness that I had been with Gavin on the mountain instead of at the house alone.

We looked over at Madi as she started to moan and move about. Like she was trying to fight someone off of her. She growled deep in her throat.

"It's okay Madi, you're safe. We have you and you are going to be okay." My mom held her thrashing hand and spoke softly to her until Madi stopped moving. I watched helplessly, wondering what had happened.

The night passed slowly, the ticking clock loud in the silence between the growling and moaning of Madi. My mom stayed with her the whole night. I slept fitfully in the armchair waking every time Madi moved about. Gavin and Apollo spent the night outside on the porch making sure no unwanted visitors showed up. When the sun peeked over the horizon, we heard the chirping of the birds. I opened my tired eyes to see Madi sitting up and talking quietly with my mom.

"Mom? Madi are you okay?" I groggily asked.

"Morning Lis." My mom came over and kissed the top of my head and went into the kitchen. I heard her rummaging about, most likely making a pot of coffee.

"Hey, Lis. I'm okay. Just a little banged up but you will learn that we heal much quicker than a human does. Even broken bones heal. Broken hearts not as fast though." Her voice trembled at the last.

"What happened?" I questioned.

"I guess Kadz wasn't the life mate for me. After I went home yesterday, I went to see him at the apartment he stayed in. It was empty. Nothing was there. It was as if he just vanished. I tried to call him, but his phone said the number had been disconnected. I don't know where he is. I was so sad I lay on the bed and cried. I fell asleep thinking I could smell him on the pillow. Lame. I woke up when the door crashed open, I was dragged into a vehicle. I didn't see who it was, but they were strong. One of them conked me on the head and I passed out. When I came around, I was in the desert, hands tied, and a blindfold covered my eyes. I don't know what they gave me, but I was not able to change form, I was just a regular teenage human girl. Quite helpless." She stopped and looked into my eyes. "Lis, they said you were next. They questioned me about you and asked all kinds of questions. I told them what I knew. I was so scared. They dragged me by my hair and took turns slapping me, I tried to change, and they laughed at me. I was humiliated. I was angry, I was scared. They cut my hair with scissors. Then they told me they were going to put me in a hole, and I was going to rot in it. I got out of the ties that held my hands and that's when they really hurt me. I must have blacked out because I woke up and I was alone. They didn't retie my hands or put me in a hole, but I didn't know where I was, and I'm still not sure what they gave me, but I can't change. I don't even know if I'm still a lycanthrope. I think they thought I was dead. I don't know why they would have left me there. They would have known that I would warn you, that I wouldn't let them harm you. You know that right Lis? I wouldn't let anyone, or anything hurt you."

I watched her bow her head and she sniffled. We were just teenagers. I smelled the coffee my mom had brewed. In a second, she was in the living room with two fresh hot cups of caffeine. I gratefully took mine and sipped on it while my mom gave a cup to Madi. She sniffed it wearily and closed her eyes a moment to remember that we were safe, she could accept a drink from us without worrying that it was poisoned. She slowly sipped the hot drink, and I watched as her pale skin pinkened up. She would be okay, physically at least.

"Madi, do you remember any other details?" I questioned her

"I told your mom everything I could remember. It isn't a lot, is it?" she quietly said as she looked at my mom.

We looked up as Gavin and Apollo entered the room.

"Madi, you look better," Gavin said as he stepped closer to my seat.

"Thank you, Gavin, for helping me," Madi answered.

"Madi, let's get you cleaned up properly. You can have a shower and borrow something from Lis. Then you need to call your parents and let them know that you are all right. Tell them you stayed late for Lis's birthday and fell asleep watching old movies with us." my mom said, and she helped Madi stand up.

"Okay." Madi let herself be led to the bathroom.

"Lis, are you okay? You have been through so much the last few days. I missed your birthday yesterday. Happy 18th Birthday." Apollo spoke in his deep voice.

"Thank you, Apollo, and yes, I'm fine. I would like to know what happened to Madi and why someone is out to hurt me. I have no enemies, none that I know of. I spoke with Kadz at the night meeting, and he told me he was going to leave but he didn't seem mad at me. He was sad. Madi said she told her kidnappers everything. That I was the leader, the Ultima. Would someone hurt my family to hurt me, Apollo?" I questioned. "Is my mom in danger because of me and the choice I made?"

"We don't know much right now, Lis but we will look into everything. You need to take precautions when you go out. It's almost time for your school bus. Would you prefer to drive yourself today? That way if anything happens you have a vehicle to leave with."

"I've been meaning to talk to you about a vehicle Apollo." I started. "The one we have now hardly makes it into town every day. It is not safe. It makes noises that cars should not make. How can I afford a new one? I also will need a vehicle when I go to University. I know Gavin says that I don't need to attend school, but it is what I want to do." I avoided looking at Gavin when I heard his low growl.

"Of course, you need a vehicle, as a matter of fact, I got you one for your birthday, Lis." Apollo smiled and reached into his pocket for a set of keys. "Your mom said you wouldn't need a new vehicle, but I thought you should have one, not only are you new to the Lycanthrope world, as well as the Ultima but you're also an adult now. There are so many reasons to celebrate you. You're mom will not be happy with me once again." He sighed as he said that, but I knew he was barely containing his happiness as he dropped the shiny new keys into my hand.

"Wow," I smiled brightly and leaned in to hug him. "Thank you, Apollo, for everything."

"You're welcome, Lis. You deserve it. It's not every day that we get an Ultima in the world. Happy Birthday." He held me a moment longer as he breathed in my scent. "You girls better be on your way. Gavin will go with you and wait for you to finish the day. Don't leave the school once you get there. I will have some of the others there as well."

"Okay," I said as I pulled away from him.

I went into the kitchen to grab a quick lunch for Madi and myself, Gabe would be sad to see half his lunch missing. I thought smiling to myself.

"Absolutely not, Apollo. No." I heard my mom.

"It's already done, Rhea. You wouldn't want her traveling on the road between school and home in an old unreliable vehicle. It's a gift, from me. Let me have this one gift, please." I heard Apollo's deep voice as it rumbled in the next room.

"You know he would give you anything if you asked for it. I would too." Gavin whispered in my ear.

I jumped a bit; I hadn't heard him follow me into the kitchen.

"It's too soon, Gavin. I told you. I need to find me first."

"I know, but I didn't say I wouldn't woo you as you searched." He grinned. He trailed his hand through my hair as I packaged up the sandwiches and grabbed some apples from the counter.

"Need some help in here?" Madi asked from the doorway.

"Nope. Lunches are ready and if you're ready to go to school we should be on our way."

"As ready as I will be. I'm a little scared, Lis. The more I think about what happened, the more pissed off I get. What if I change at school? What if I get so mad, that I start ripping people apart? What if I can't control the rage that is rippling inside me? My wolf is mad, I can feel her banging to get free and find the people who hurt me. It would only take me a second to let her out, I'm scared that if I did that, then I wouldn't be able to pull her back in." Madi stood silently gripping the door jamb.

"Madi, listen to me. You have been a werewolf for years. You have grown with her inside you, and you have kept her in control. Even when your human hormones were going nuts. You kept her in control. You let your wolf run and she knew her limits. Right now, she is pushing you and her limits, you have to give her some room, but you can't let her rule you. You are still in control. Don't shut her out but don't let her win either. Keep your cool head. We will figure this out together, that is what it means to belong to a pack. You belong to my pack Madi. You are my best friend and I need you. You need me as well. Together we can figure this out. As a part of my family, you will never, ever have to figure things out on your own again. My family, your brothers and sisters, we will all help you and we will find out who hurt you and who wants to hurt me. When we do figure it out, we will decide what to do, together. Okay?"

"Okay." Madi released a loud breath that she had been holding in, "Thanks, Lis."

"Let's get going ladies. You don't want Gabe to be standing around waiting by the bus stop for either of you." Gavin had grabbed an apple and crunched into it while steering both of us out the front door.

"Bye Mom, bye Apollo. If we need anything we can call or send Gavin." I laughed as he growled and kept pushing me out the doorway. "Thank you for the present Apollo. My mom will forgive you." I yelled as we went down the stairs towards the new, black Jeep sitting in the driveway.

The ride to school went swiftly and we laughed while the wind rushed through our hair. It was like running through the mountains.

"Madi, I will be outside within hearing distance. You just need to think of my name, and I will hear you. Okay." Gavin reminded her as we turned the corner and saw the yellow school buses start their lineup.

"Okay." She sounded a bit nervous still.

"Come on Madi." I looked over at her as we parked and grabbed our bags. "Gabe will be wondering where you are. He's usually the first one here."

"Be aware of your surroundings ladies. Remember to call if you need me. I will be staying in town all day." Gavin gripped my arm before I could leap from the jeep. "I mean in Lis. Don't think you can handle this alone. It might not be anyone from this world. There are others out there and they happen to find this world sometimes and don't want to leave it. There are dangerous beings out there. Be careful today." His brow furrowed as he thought about leaving us all day.

"I will be fine Gavin. So will Madi. See you later." I smiled gently at him in reassurance and closed the car door.

Without turning back, I led Madi toward the sputtering busses.

I saw Madi look over her shoulder as the jeep drove away. I gripped her hand and she turned to me.

"It's going to be okay Madi. You're safe and I'm safe. Let's just get through today one hour at a time. If you need me just call me in your mind, and I will hear you. Let's go now."

We walked slowly towards the loud busses which had students pouring out of the doors. We saw Gabe's bus and headed towards it. We saw him before he saw us. He looked sick, really sick.

"Hey, Gabe. Are you okay? You look really sick, should you even be at school today?" I asked him as we walked a step towards the school.

"I feel okay today, I just haven't slept very well the last couple of days. I can't even eat. But I don't have a fever, so Mom said school it is. I really need to get that scholarship, or I won't be able to attend school full-time in the fall." He said as we walked into the cool shade of the school building.

"You should get it, Gabe, you need it," I said.

"So do you, Lis. I know that. We promised we would be happy for each other remember. You're awfully quiet today Madi, everything alright?" he questioned her.

"Yup, everything is going to be fine." Madi looked from me to Gabe as she answered. "Hey look, the bell is going to go in a minute, I have to get to class. See you at lunch." She waved as she turned and headed down the hallway to her first class.

"Is she really Okay, Lis? She didn't look Okay." Gabe asked me, concern dripping off of every word.

"Gabe, relax. Madi is fine. You should ask her to prom. She's been waiting for you to ask."

"What about you?" he questioned. "I don't want to ask her and have you go solo. What about if we all went together like we do everything? Hey Lis, I'm sorry for acting like a jerk the other day. I need you as my friend too. You know I like you both, but I think something has changed between me and Madi. Well, it has for me anyway." He hung his head in a bashful way and his cheeks went a little bit pink.

I smiled; he was a great friend. "Gabe, I know you thought you liked me like a girlfriend, but we are more like siblings, so it's okay. No need to apologize. Madi likes you too, but she is a little distracted today. Like I said, ask her to prom. I think I have my date. Come on." I hurried as I heard the bell start to ring loudly.

In the waning sounds of the school bell, I swear I heard a baby cry.

CHAPTER TWENTY-SEVEN
The Baby

I was distracted throughout the school day. Waiting for the kidnappers to make an appearance. Trying to figure out why I was the only one to hear a baby crying. Wondering about Gavin and our non-relationship. The Valedictorian speech I still had to write and even wonder if I would be chosen after all the absences I had lately. Maybe Gabe should be the recipient, after all, I now knew that I had the resources to go to school. I just had to ask Apollo, maybe even ask Gavin although he thought school would be a waste of time. Lunch was uneventful. Gabe did ask why we had the same sandwiches, so we had to give him an edited version of the previous night's events. We didn't have to tell him about the kidnapping or the beating that Madi had endured, she had healed up and her appearance looked fine.

I heard Gavin's heartbeat from across the field and stopped myself from going to him. He was only there for our protection. I needed to keep my mind on school.

The final bell of the day seemed to take forever. I wondered how Madi had done it. Kept her secret for so long. The call to let my wolf run free was overwhelming. I had to excuse myself from class this afternoon when I felt my wolf try to get out. Gabe had looked at me funny and I knew my eyes had changed color. I told him it was just a flash of the lights. I knew my wolf wanted out just to find the crying baby. I wanted it too.

We said goodbye to Gabe as he boarded the bus and found Gavin as he sat parked in the student parking lot waiting for us.

"I need to get home. My mom is a little mad that I didn't get home last night. Thanks for being close by today, Gavin. It helped me get through the day. Did you guys figure out anything yet? I mean do we know why Lis was the target?" Madi grilled Gavin as we settled into the Jeep.

Distractedly, I looked out the window as I heard the wailing baby. Gavin and Madi were just mumbling in the background. In moments we were outside Madi's house, and I told her to call me tonight. Sooner if she remembered anything else or needed us for anything.

"You're distracted, Lis, what's going on in that head of yours?" Gavin asked as we drove out to my place.

"I hear the baby crying again. What is it? My wolf almost jumped out today during class when I heard it. I need to find out what it is. Where it is. Who it is. It sounds like they need me, well I think it's my werewolf that is getting called." I whispered. "I need to find out who needs me. That's part of my job in leading the lycanthropes, right? To come when I am being called."

"Let's go for a run when we drop the Jeep off. We can run to Apollo's and see what he knows about the crying baby." Gavin reassured me.

"Okay," I answered softly.

The rest of the drive home was made in silence. Except for the crying. I could feel my heart rip in despair as I listened to the tiny wails. I closed my eyes and concentrated on keeping my wolf quiet.

As we rounded the long drive to my house, I heard a loud roar. Startled I looked over at Gavin and saw that his eyes were round, and he whipped his head forward and floored the gas pedal making my head snap back against the seat.

He was halfway out the door before the truck stopped rolling and bounded up the front stairs before he ripped open the old wooden door. It slapped noisily against the wall before it closed again. I raced behind him to open the door and yelled out for my mom. Silence greeted me. I raced upstairs to her room and knew before I opened it that she wasn't in there. Who had made that terrible scream? It was like someone had their heart torn out.

"Lis!" Gavin yelled out. "We need to go, now. We need to get back to town. Apollo needs me."

I sprinted back down the stairs and saw the front door slam shut as Gavin raced outside. I heard his howl as I reached the front door. Okay, going to town would be faster if I changed. I closed my eyes and changed. It was that easy. I hardly had to think about it.

Hopefully, my clothes would be intact when we got to town. I leapt off the porch and stretched my legs to catch up to Gavin who was already down the driveway.

What's going on Gavin? I asked as I reached his side.

Apollo called everyone, something big is happening. You might get to meet my family sooner rather than later. He answered.

I could hear the concern in his voice. I could tell he was anxious. He didn't know what we were going to face once we reached town.

Is my mom okay Gavin? I asked.

So far as I can tell, she is fine. So is Apollo.

We were almost to the edge of town by that time. It had taken us mere minutes to race across the distance, the light of the town streetlights grew brighter as we approached. We slowed down a minute to sniff the air and listen to the sounds. I heard the baby crying, wait a minute, there was more than one. What was happening? I stole a glance at Gavin, his shoulders were tense, eyes iced blue. He had his Beta eyes. Something was very wrong. I could feel it. My she-wolf wanted to howl, to call everyone. I pushed the urge down. We needed to be quiet.

So many babies, why are they all crying? I asked as I looked at Gavin.

Those are the cries you have been hearing. Gavin turned to look at me sharply.

Yes, you can hear them too. I questioned him back. I was glad he could hear them; it gave me comfort to know I wasn't going crazy, I almost wept out loud with relief.

Lis, the cries are unborn werewolves, and from what I can tell they are inside the humans. The humans who do not know they are lycanthropes. The babies are werewolves who are trying to come out. Our town is now full of unborn werewolves. A whole town. I need to find Apollo; this is not natural. You were supposed to be the only human-born lycanthrope.

I gasped. *Did I do this? Did I think about how better my life would be if the whole town knew our secret?*

Lis, you didn't do this. It's not that easy to make a new lycanthrope. The gods can do it, we have done it multiple times in fact. It takes time to change the world and make new lives out of nothing. I could hear the censor in his voice.

I forgot easily, Gavin and Apollo were Gods. They had made this world; they were not supposed to interfere in the human world anymore. They wanted to live like humans and have human lives here. They finished building this world hundreds of years ago. Why was it changing now and why were they surprised by the change? They were supposed to know all the answers. They were supposed to give choices to the humans and go from there. The humans were supposed to have free will. It sounded to me like Gavin still wanted to control everyone and everything in this world. Why would he be scared to know that there were more lycanthropes than they thought there should be? At the back of my mind, the thought that pushed everything else away came through hard. I might meet Gavin's family. The gods who had created this world. I hope my clothes were intact.

Should we change? I asked Gavin.

Yes, some of the others are here already. They are at the school. Let's get a bit closer before we change. It's easier to hear and smell as a lycanthrope. Come on.

We crept closer toward the main road staying along the old brick buildings, silently listening to the cries that called to one another. I could hear the difference now, they had changed, the town was full of werewolves, and they had no idea what had happened to them. They were scared, confused, and starting to panic. I wanted to go to them, I wanted to call them to me. I could help them. I just knew they needed me or maybe I needed them. Just then we saw Madi walking upright. Why wasn't she a wolf? She could be hurt again. I darted behind a big garbage bin and changed, miraculously I had my clothes on. No rips or tears either.

"Madi? Madi." I whispered loudly.

I waited till she spotted me by the dumpster and headed my way. Gavin had crept up behind me still as a werewolf, but I heard him change and adjust his clothing properly.

"What are you doing?" I asked her quietly.

"I had to come here, at first it was just a feeling in my gut, then I heard a scream, and I started running but I was scared to change so it took me a bit longer to get to town, I heard babies crying, like a lot of babies. It's strange and my wolf is quivering inside me. She wants out badly. What is going on?"

"The cries are baby lycanthropes; we don't know why there are so many of them," Gavin told her as she stood beside me. "we have to get to the school and stay together. Let's move."

"Madi, there might be some stuff you don't understand but just trust Gavin and me, okay? We won't let anything happen to you." I tried to give Madi a little warning about meeting Gavin's family. I was a little apprehensive as well, but I trusted Gavin to keep me safe.

The school building came into view, and we stopped to gather information before we went ahead. I could hear loud voices inside.

"It's okay, it's just my family. They are here already." Gavin tugged my hand and I grabbed Madi's. Together the three of us climbed the familiar stairs and Gavin held the door open. He had a smile on his face, but I felt apprehension. What would they think of me? The new Ultima, the person they had given the choice to lead all the lycanthropes or be human. Would they like me? Would I be the person they thought I would be? Strong enough? Loyal enough? Brave enough? I wasn't sure I was any of those things.

In moments we were at the doors to the gym. I took a deep relaxing breath and blew it out slowly. It didn't matter if they liked me or not, I repeated in my mind, Gavin liked me enough. I wasn't sure if I could do any of this without him. I looked at him and saw a side of him I didn't know. He looked happy but sad at the same time. I saw him straighten his shoulders and clear his mind. He didn't know about his family either. That was strange.

The first person I saw was an exceptionally large native-looking man, with gloriously long black hair braided and tied at the end with a leather strip. Beside him, holding tightly to his rather large hand was a beautiful blond lady, she couldn't be more than five years older than me. She was looking adoringly up at the man beside her. Her eyes were a beautiful shade of blue. They belonged together; they must be the newlyweds Gavin had told me about. Tyler and Ava. She turned to us and eyed Gavin with uncertainty before she looked at me with curiosity. She gave me a small smile before looking back at Tyler.

"Gavin, you're finally here. Always late little brother. I had to open a rather large gate this morning, some unsavory types were here looking to take over the world, one ultima at a time. They had been bragging about kidnapping one of your wolves earlier. Everything okay with that?" I heard another equally tall brother, who had dark red hair and green eyes drawl. He sounded so superior, that I had to fight the urge to correct him. A petite curly-haired girl stepped on his toe, I laughed at his expression, he must be Ian and the pretty dark-haired girl would be Enid, the new goddess.

"Well, it's not a party unless I'm invited. We had a little bit of trouble the other day, thank you for taking care of it for us. " Gavin answered curtly, "Hello brothers and sisters. This is our new Ultima, Lis, and her Zeta, Madi. Madi was the unfortunate one who was beaten badly by her kidnappers; however, she is recovering nicely as you can all see."

I looked at Madi who looked around her with her mouth open. We were in the presence of Gods. I felt exactly how she looked. Speechless. As I took in the rest of the group looking at us, I remembered that I was holding Gavin's hand, tightly, and it hadn't gone unnoticed by the group standing before us. I also held tightly in my other hand my best friend's hand. I let go of their hands and stepped forward.

"It's a pleasure to meet you all and I look forward to talking and getting to know each of you better. However, right now I need to know why you have made so many new unborn werewolves in this town. If I am really the Ultima you have made me, I need answers. Now." I looked at each of the eyes that were glaring at me and watched as they flickered to Madi and Gavin and back to me. They all looked at each other and finally, a silent act was decided among them.

"Lis, nice to finally meet you. We didn't make the lycanthropes. They are a product of this world. Your world." His voice slid like silk over my mind, Tyler, he was the newlywed.

"Lis, these babies, the new lycanthropes, they are your pack. You need to gather and teach. It is why you were given the role, the choice." Ian, the redhead, with the cold green eyes, spoke softly. Like I was a child he had to console. I didn't care for his tone at all.

"You made me make a choice, and I accept my decision, but I have no idea what they need, want, or crave. A whole town of wolves, all of them will be scared. You do hear their cries, right?" I snapped right back at him. "Last night my Zeta was attacked and left on my doorstep, do any of you know why the kidnappers did that? The message they left her with was that I would be next, and I wouldn't be as lucky as she was." I paused to let that sink in and watched as they all looked at Madi with new eyes. "If you didn't make the new lycanthropes and I didn't make them who else would have that type of power? And are they a new army sent to harm me and my human family or my pack family? Do any of you have a reasonable answer for that?"

I watched as Ian grew taller, right before my eyes.

"You question us? You dare to take that tone with us?" His green eyes frosted over, and his red hair looked like it was going to start on fire.

Gavin grabbed my hand, and I looked back at him and Madi. He would fight them for me, he tried to pull me behind him, and I watched as he started to grow as well. He couldn't do this. They had made me the Ultima for a reason, I think I was starting to understand why. This family had no communication skills.

I looked up at the frosted green eyes and tore my hand from Gavin's. Tyler was looking at Gavin in fascination. A small smile curved his lips as he watched me step forward. Maybe he would be an ally in the near future.

"Ian. Yes, I question you, all of you. We are family. I am new to this family, and I don't like to disappoint anyone. If you haven't made the wolves then we need to find out who did, and fighting among ourselves will not get it done. Apollo isn't here. Do any of you know where he is, I am asking because anywhere he goes his Luna, my mother, will follow, and I am really worried about her. You are here to help right?" I questioned the group and the girls nodded and smiled at me, the Gods just grunted, and Ian calmed down enough to shrink back to human size, his green eyes turning to normal once again.

"I knew we were going to like you, Lis," Ava said as she looked at me with acceptance in her eyes.

I gave a startled gasp as we all felt the walls of the high school gym rattle.

"What was that?" Madi questioned out loud.

"Let's find out what's keeping Apollo," Tyler said as we looked alarmingly at the locked doors that rattled like someone was trying to break in.

"It's nothing, just some humans trying to break in and find out what's going on here," Ian mumbled to Enid.

"That doesn't sound like human sounds." She replied loudly.

The gym quieted suddenly, and we could all hear our breathing echoing in the large area. What was going on?

"I need to find my mom. I'm going to the mountain." I said to Gavin.

"They aren't on the mountain Lis. I don't know where they are. It's like they are being cloaked. Something is breaking our communication with each other. Has anyone heard or spoken to Apollo in the last twenty minutes?" Gavin asked his family. My heart sank as I watched their heads shake in the negative.

"Okay" Gavin spoke, once more in control, "Okay, I know they aren't on the mountain, which is our usual meeting spot. They aren't at the cabin; I can see it and it's empty. The hospital is off-limits as the humans inside are incapacitated, they aren't there. We just left the farmhouse and it's empty as well."

The doors to the gymnasium shook again and we all heard the howls coming from outside.

"We have to figure this out on our own. Apollo is safe, I think, as is Rhea. Tyler, would you open the doors to the gym? You have a connection to the animals that we don't, even if they are werewolves. Lis, Madi, and I will be behind you. They are looking for Lis. I'm sure of it. Ian, Enid, and Ava will stand beside us and try to keep them from loading in here. The one at the door will be the leader, even if they are lone wolves, they will feel like they should be listening to one member. I'm not sure about this but it's the best we have right now. If we wait any longer, they will find their way in here and we won't have the advantage. Ian and Tyler, the Lycanthropes are different than what we had meant them for, they are strong but obedient. Right now, they are new, they are strong, and they are very confused. Lis will need to take control once we have the pack leader ready to listen. Are you all ready?"

As one, we nodded our affirmation. We moved in unison to flank the double doors to the gym, now quiet. Tyler moved to the front after kissing his new bride atop her blonde head. She was new to this family, like me. My stomach trembled as I watched Tyler lift his bronze hand to the steel handle and push it down and outward. We held our breath a second before the door flew open and a rather large black wolf entered the room. Kadzait.

TWENTY-EIGHT

Lis's Court

Stunned by the appearance of the wolf that had willingly left the pack we watched as a pack of wolves, fully grown entered the gym behind him. They stopped as they made the V formation. Kadz was clearly their leader.

"Kadz?" Madi whispered his name.

He looked at her longingly for seconds before he turned his yellow gaze to Gavin and me. He was hardly taking in the other occupants of the room. He felt he deserved to be in command. I could feel it. He was trying to take my place as Ultima. I growled low and deep in my throat. I was still human, so the sound didn't hit the notes I tried for.

"Kadzait, nice to see you once again. Why have you come back to this town? You physically hurt Madi. Are you here to hurt me now?" I asked out loud. "Why have you brought all these new Lycanthropes to us? They are scared. You're scaring them, they should be human not werewolf. Kadz, please let them go. Let them be human again." I stepped around Gavin and kept Madi as hidden as I could. Tyler stood beside me still as a statue. "Kadzait, it's just you and me, we don't need the others. Come on, let's talk." I tried my best to sound like I was asking him to do me a favor, not demanding that he listen. I had to try, I knew he loved Madi, he had looked confused when I said he had hurt her. Maybe he wasn't the one behind her kidnapping and torture.

"I came back to lead the packs with you Lis, I didn't hurt Madi, I could never hurt her. The three of us belong together. We can lead the packs together. We don't have to be life mates; you were right about that. You only chose Gavin as a mate because he didn't give you a choice. I was with you, I helped you when you needed it, and I was there when you first changed. We have a link that cannot be broken. The town, this town of werewolves is ready to be led by us. We will be the largest, strongest pack in the world. I have been to the far corners of this large world, and you are needed, Lis. You will need a family large enough to keep the packs in line. I have given you this family. We are ready to join you."

I was the only one who heard this conversation. I knew Gavin could tell we were speaking but I didn't get the feeling he knew exactly the words that Kadz spoke.

"Kadzait." I paused a moment. This answer needed to be what he needed to hear, or else war would ensue. I was sure our side would win, but the casualties would be too much. I deliberately spoke aloud so everyone could hear me. "Kadz, I have a family." I looked around at the people who supported me. He finally looked around at the new people he hadn't met before. He stopped and met the gazes of

Ian and Tyler who although looked nothing like Gavin you knew they were brothers. It was in their stance. They looked like statues while Kadz evaluated them one by one. None of them moved a muscle, they were waiting for my command, my lead. It was a test. From the Gods. I knew it.

"Kadzait, let me meet the new pack members. Let's have a talk before any decisions are made. I am the Ultima, they are my pack members whether they stay here or move away, they should all meet me and know who I am and who my family is." I sensed a shuffle in the pack and watched as a tall, younger pack member walked in. Kadz tried to stop them, but they only stopped as they came before me. I knew those eyes, those kind but confused eyes.

"Gabe?" I questioned him softly. "It's going to be okay; we got your back."

Gabe was larger than most, his coat was bright blond and his grey eyes looked like he understood what was going on. He looked from me to Gavin and then to Madi, he hung his head and gave it a little shake. I knew he was disappointed in us. We had left him out of our trust, he was our best friend and we had excluded him. I felt horrible, I knew he was the one who had been crying, he was who I had heard for the past few days. He needed us and we had left him out in the cold. I knew we would be having a long talk later on. Suddenly he stood up tall and howled. Gavin stepped forward as did Ian, but I shook my head at them. Gabe needed to be heard. The pack that had been converged at the doors parted as a group of young werewolves walked in, some were bouncing like playful puppies—his team. Gabe had brought his football team together. I looked at him as he bowed low to me and barked at the football team, they bowed low to me as they entered and stood behind Ian, Ava, and Enid. He had our backs too. I watched as he winked at Madi and passed her to stand with his mates. Barking at them to settle down.

We stepped back to let the others enter. Most were confused, stumbling on their four legs. The remaining pack members knew they should be bowing to me, but they were confused to see Katz there. They didn't know what to do and some members started crying, I could see and feel their frustration and confusion. The seven of us moved as one taking up the centre-court line at the gymnasium. Ian and Tyler each took a spot at the end. Gavin and Madi flanked me on either side and beside each of them stood Ava and Enid. The football team and Gabe stood just behind us, guarding our backs. I looked at them all and gave a silent thanks. I took a step forward and began.

"Hello everyone. I know you are confused and maybe a bit scared as well. My friend, Kadzait, has asked you all here to talk with me. My name is Lis, and I am sure some of you know me from around town. I have lived here in this town almost all my life. I have attended school with your kids, and we are friends with lots of you. Madi and Gabe are my best friends, you know us. You have watched them play sports, congratulated them on their wins, and accepted them as one of your own, our town heroes. We are still those people, but we are more as well. We are Lycanthropes or werewolves. You knew we lived here. Deep down you knew we were a part of your town and you let us be. We didn't bother you then and we won't now. Our families have never needed to be divided, today you were brought here without your permission. You weren't asked if you wanted to be werewolves, and I apologize for that." I paused and I looked slowly at Kadz. "I will give you all the chance now to choose. If you would like to stay and be a pack member you are free to do so. We are a quiet community; we don't harm others if we can help it. We like to be outdoors, and we like to run in the mountains and feel the fresh air brush our faces. We will help you if you need it. We will teach you our rules and the hierarchy that this life encompasses. You will always have a family if you stay a werewolf. However, if you don't choose this life I will change you back to human, only human. You will not remember this life or the people who choose to remain werewolves. We will still be your human friends and co-workers, but you won't know about us. You might have dreams that werewolves exist, but you won't be afraid. This is your choice. Choose wisely, I will only offer this choice here and now. If you choose to be a lycanthrope with all the pack rules, please leave this building and gather on the football field. We will be there and explain further our roles to you once we have sent the humans home. If you choose to be human once more, please stay and my brother, Ian, will talk you back to human form and help you forget that we exist. Go now. Choose wisely."

I walked over to Kadz and looked him in the eyes, I spoke low and commanding. "Stay Kadz, we will talk." I didn't give him a choice.

I walked over to Gabe and squatted down. "Hey, sorry. We should have told you. Even if you decide to be human, I will still tell you. Okay?" I smiled as he gave me a little headbutt and barked at his team. One by one they moved past me each one bowing low before they exited the building and headed out to the football field. A few more exited without giving it too much thought. In less than a minute the choices had been made. There were only a handful of new weres left in the gym. The majority had left and were waiting on the field. Katz and his new band of wolves sat together and waited quietly. Tyler watched over them to make sure they didn't bully any of the new wolves to move outside.

"Okay, Ian. Would you make sure these people return to their previous lives unhindered by our presence? Could you give them something to be happy about as well? They will be reminded of us in their night dreams, let their daytimes be something cheerful to offset that."

"I can see to that. Enid, stay with me. This is something we try to avoid as much as possible. There could be consequences that we didn't anticipate."

They walked hand in hand toward the litter of puppies who were somber and waited to be turned back into humans.

"Lis?" Ian turned to look at me. "Would you like to be included in this group? We don't usually give second chances, but you have proven that you are brave and a born leader. Human or Lycanthrope you will be a leader in this world. I will grant you this one chance if you want it."

Gavin stood up and took a step towards his older brother but thought better of it and looked back at me instead.

"Lis?" I heard the question in his voice.

Did I want this? Did I want to go back to being human? I thought about the path of my human life, Valedictorian, schooling, life, and kids. Did I want that? The choice was mine. My mom and I could turn our backs on this whole life and go back to normal—just the two of us. We wouldn't have to worry about all the lycanthropes in the world. It could be just us once more.

"Thank you for giving me the choice Ian, but I choose this life. I choose my Lycanthrope family; I choose Gavin as my life mate, and I choose all of you as my family. I wouldn't give up anything. I am happy to be a leader and I am happy that you chose me. So no, Ian, I will not stay inside and change back to human. I love who I am, and I am happy with all of you. I always wanted a family and now I have an exceptionally large extended one. I have to get outside now my family is waiting for me. Madi, Gavin I would like to make Gabe my Beta. He is the most loyal person I have ever met and he's our best friend Madi. We shouldn't have kept this from him."

"As you wish Lis," Ian answered.

"Whatever you decide is fine with me." Madi chimed in.

"Beta?" Gavin questioned.

"You are my mate Gavin, not my Beta. When I need to leave, you will be by my side, not staying behind to support the pack in my absence. We are one and I won't ever be alone again."

"Okay," he smiled "let's go support our new family before the sun rises. There's also someone outside who eagerly wants to speak with you."

"One more thing before we leave." I motioned to Kadz and took a step closer to him and his pack.

"Kadzait," I called to him "come here. Stand up and talk with me." The timber in my voice gave him no choice.

He started to walk on all fours and as he reached me, he had grown taller and soon he stood before me as a human. I remember why I had been drawn to him. He oozed confidence and we both knew he could be a great leader.

"Kadz, I would welcome you back into the pack if you wanted that. I would also welcome your group of bodyguards. You would be bound by all the same rules as every new member, no favoritism. You have tried to hurt our members; you have turned innocent humans into werewolves just to get a band together with the intent to hurt us. Please don't deny it. I know everything you have done, and everything you wanted to accomplish. I can read it in your thoughts." I paused; I knew Gavin was listening to every word. "Kadz, I will also give you the option that Ian just gave me. I give you the choice to be human again."

In my mind, I could hear Gavin screech at me. He was not happy with the choices I had given Kadz. I knew that they would never see eye to eye, some people were never meant to get along and they were a fine example.

"You would take me back?" Kadz asked. "Only as a new member though. I would be nothing. I have worked my way up in Apollos pack for years, and it would all be for nothing. I would belong as a part of a rather large pack but be a middleman with no authority. Or I could be human again. I barely remember what it is like to be human. No pack to have my back. It's a lonely life, to be human but I'm still young, I could find a mate and have my own human family."

I watched him for a moment as he considered his two options. He looked at Madi and walked over to her and whispered in her ear. Then I watched as he hugged her and kissed her forehead before he stood before me once more.

"I choose to be human again. It's time for me to live my life for me now. Thank you, Lis, for giving me the choice. I know you will be a great Ultima and I am sorry that I have caused you and your new family so much trouble."

I watched as he let the decision wash over him, he smiled a radiant smile, and then I knew what Madi had seen in him. He would be a kind human; he would defend the helpless and he would protect his human family.

"Go Kadz, be happy. Your choice has been made. Ian will help you out." My heart felt lighter as I watched him shrug his shoulders at the pack of bodyguards he was leaving behind. I felt sorry for them.

"Kadz has decided that being all human with no knowledge of the lycanthrope world is what he wants. You all have three seconds to choose as well. Outside now, if you want to be a part of my pack family or stay in the gym where Ian will help you be all human with no knowledge of us once more."

They scrambled in their haste, bumping into each other as half of them ran outside and the other half ran to where Kadz was standing by Ian.

"Okay Ian, it's sorted now." I looked at my family, the mixture that every human family had. My family. "Let's head to the field and start teaching. Madi, you need to grab Gabe and half the group while Gavin and I take the other half. Tyler, Ava, would you take a handful of the youngest members? They will need more instruction than most. Let's start from the top. Let them know they are loved and that they will never be alone again; they are now a part of our family, and we will protect them all."

As we exited the gym, I heard Ian start gathering the scared new lycanthropes and begin telling them a story. He started by telling them they were in a dream. The heavy doors behind us closed with a loud snap.

I sucked in a huge breath and blew it out loudly. I needed to clear my head. I had to forget the people in the gymnasium and focus my energy on the ones waiting for me on the football field.

Madi, Gavin, Tyler, Ava, and I walked out together arm in arm. We let out a collective gasp as we saw my mother and Apollo talking with Gabe. They stood with their backs to us and turned together as they heard us approach.

"Mom?" I asked, "Apollo? Where have you guys been? We were all so worried." I wrapped my arms around my mom as I questioned them.

With her arms wrapped around me tightly my mom answered first. "We had to leave. I didn't want to go but Apollo made me, I didn't have a choice."

"Apollo? What? Explain." I looked over at him.

"Lis, you look beautiful, exactly how I knew you could. We were holding you back, you needed to make decisions on your own without constantly looking to your mom to help you out. She was holding on to you as well," he sighed as he looked at her still hugging me tightly. "You changed so fast, and you adapted so easily however you struggled to see who you wanted to be in the end. The Ultima, the leader or the Valedictorian, the human. I am glad you have chosen the pack. You are a born leader. You know about us, and you embraced us, chastised us, and believed in us. You were the right choice to lead this pack around the world, this world, and you are the right person to fit into this family."

"Thank you, Apollo." I swallowed the lump in my throat at his praise. I hadn't known I needed to hear it until now. "This world?" I questioned him softly.

"Lis, you know I am not just a surgeon. I am needed in other worlds, and I need your mom. I need her. Today we had to help Tim Herrin decide where he wanted to go, he needed to decide to stay here with his loving family who have been with him daily in the hospital or he could go on to the next world and continue his life there. He needed to hear that we all have choices, and they won't always be good choices. He had a hard one to make and it is hard on me to give these choices. Your mom helps me, she brings balance to my life that I didn't know I needed. You will do great, and Gavin needs you now. I am so proud of the woman you have grown into. We are both so proud of you.

"Lis, Apollo, and I are going to go for a little while. We will be close by; Ian will help us travel to each other. Those doors will always be open for us to visit, anytime you need me, us." My mom looked up at me with her arms still holding me close to her.

"You're leaving me?" I whispered while my eyes filled with unshed tears.

"Not leaving you, believing in you." She said.

"We need to go Rhea. It's time." Apollo interrupted.

"Mom?" I questioned her.

"You are brave Lis; you have a formidable team. The pack is waiting for your direction. Bring them together, trust in them and they will trust you. You did the right thing for Katz, now go do the same for all these lycanthropes waiting for you, and by the way, Gabe is going to be a great Beta, you have chosen well. I am so proud of you. You are exactly where you need to be right now. Love Gavin, show him how love can be good. He needs you too. Be strong and stand your ground, the Gods can be a bit demanding, trust me." She rolled her eyes and smiled.

I would miss her. We watched as they walked away from us, she turned to wave just as they disappeared. My breath caught and I felt Gavin squeeze my hand gently. I looked at him and smiled. I took a deep breath and turned to face my court.

It was my time to start teaching.

EPILOGUE

Finally, we smiled as we watched the striking girl take command. Neither of us could deny the love we saw shining in our youngest son's eyes as he watched his Ultima, his mate.

Our children were going to be okay in this world we had all created, I looked lovingly at my beautiful wife. We had done well. Our children, the Gods we had lovingly shaped, were going to be just fine in this human world.

Manufactured by Amazon.ca
Bolton, ON